# Madison moved away from him

Steve sensed she was trying to build a wall between them, needing to create distance from feelings that had come on too strong too soon. He watched as she stopped in front of the television, where some ridiculous commercial about a goat and a soft drink was playing.

"You don't feel like a stranger to me," Steve said as he watched her from his vantage point by the window.

The sincerity in his voice forced Madison to turn to face him. His face was an open book, free for her to read. And in his warm brown eyes and sensual lips, she read an emotion that was greater than lust and infatuation.

"You feel like home to me," he added softly.

D1413891

**Books by Kim Shaw**

Kimani Romance

*Forever, For Always, For Love*
*Soul Caress*
*The Foreigner's Caress*

Kimani Arabesque

*Pack Light*
*Free Verse*
*Love's Portrait*

---

## KIM SHAW

is a high school English teacher in New Jersey and a student in the inaugural class of the Rutgers Newark MFA creative writing program. Between teaching, studying and spending time with her family, she continues to create stories readers love.

# The FOREIGNER'S CARESS

*Kim Shaw*

KIMANI
ROMANCE

If you purchased this book without a cover you should be aware
that this book is stolen property. It was reported as "unsold and
destroyed" to the publisher, and neither the author nor the
publisher has received any payment for this "stripped book."

 KIMANI PRESS™

ISBN-13: 978-0-373-86058-6
ISBN-10:    0-373-86058-7

THE FOREIGNER'S CARESS

Copyright © 2008 by Kimberly Sharrock Shaw

All rights reserved. The reproduction, transmission or utilization
of this work in whole or in part in any form by any electronic, mechanical
or other means, now known or hereafter invented, including xerography,
photocopying and recording, or in any information storage or retrieval
system, is forbidden without written permission. For permission please
contact Kimani Press, Editorial Office, 233 Broadway, New York, NY
10279 U.S.A.

This is a work of fiction. Names, characters, places and incidents are
either the product of the author's imagination or are used fictitiously,
and any resemblance to actual persons, living or dead, business establishments,
events or locales is entirely coincidental.

® and TM are trademarks. Trademarks indicated with ® are registered in
the United States Patent and Trademark Office, the Canadian Trade Marks
Office and/or other countries.

www.kimanipress.com

Printed in U.S.A.

Dear Reader,

Kennedy Daniels's little sister is all grown up! I hope that you enjoy watching Madison evolve into a beautiful, independent young woman who snags a sexy Englishman to call her own. Ironically, this time it's the Daniels clan who are being told that they are not *good enough*.

This is a passionate story about people who must first learn to love and trust themselves before they can do the same for each other. Madison and Steve find a love that cannot be bound by geographic or cultural limitations.

Please visit my Web site, www.kimshaw.net, for information on upcoming releases. Coming up next, I'll take you to New York City's Great White Way, where passion and the next starring role are never guaranteed.

Yours truly,

Kim Shaw

## Dedication

Over the past couple of years I have discovered the depths of the loyalty romance readers have for the writers they love. This novel is dedicated to romance readers, who continuously demand the best from the heroes, heroines and, ultimately, the writers.

# Chapter 1

"Your invitation, please?"

Madison pulled the five-by-eight-inch, eggshell cardstock invite from the silver evening bag that hung on her shoulder and handed it to the usher. She looked at him over the top of the Armani shades that sat perched on the tip of her delicate nose. He read the name embossed in gold lettering, allowing his gaze to travel from her Christian Louboutin stiletto-clad French-manicured toes, up shapely tanned legs to a hemline that ended above her knees, continuing to round hips, a tiny waist and ample cleavage. He settled on her face, an approving smile on his lips as he handed her invitation back over to her.

"Thank you, Ms. Madison Daniels. Welcome to the 'Friends to Elect the next United States President' banquet. Enjoy yourself this evening."

"I always do," Madison said.

She glided through the door the young man held open, her steps poised, her grace evident of a childhood of grooming. The wine-colored carpeted foyer to the Grand Promenade Ballroom was peppered with tuxedos and cocktail dresses as men and women chatted and laughed gaily. The backless, minuscule Donna Karan dress she wore, stunning and shimmering silver, caused passing gazes to linger on the "redbone" beauty as she made her way through the room. She was used to the attention and was undeterred as she continued to the main room, a faint scent of Armani Code perfume accentuating the air immediately around her. She stopped just inside the door, looked around, a frown forming at the corners of her mouth.

"Are you disappointed because he's here or because he's not here?" a deep voice asked from beside her.

Madison turned slowly to the left, her gaze traveling upward until it landed on a chiseled face. Gleaming white teeth set inside supple lips curved in a smile greeted her. An even-toned nutmeg face with eyes like ebony marbles framed by curly eyelashes was fixed in her direction.

"Excuse me?" she quipped.

"You were looking around for someone and your expression was one of obvious disappointment," he said.

"And naturally you assumed that I was looking for a man? Typical," Madison scoffed.

"I suppose I could not fathom that a beautiful woman such as yourself could ever be unescorted to a well-appointed affair such as this. My luck has never been quite that good, although I did win a blue ribbon at a potato sack race once when I was seven years old."

There was no doubting the charm of the debonair stranger. The unmistakably English accent was melodic to Madison's ears, making his rash judgment of her mood sound less antagonistic. He was long-drink-of-water tall, at least six feet two inches, towering above her diminutive frame. The span of his broad shoulders was visible in the classic Ralph Lauren black tuxedo he wore, and for a moment she had a fantasy of him picking her up, tossing her over one shoulder and carrying her away into his jungle lair. She snapped out of it with a quick shake of the head. She was no Jane and he certainly was no chocolate Tarzan. What he was was extremely good-looking, smooth-talking and probably the sexiest man she'd ever laid eyes on. However, Madison was not a woman who was easily charmed by good looks and sweet words.

"Look, Mr.—"

"Elliott."

"Mr. Elliott—"

"Stevenson. Stevenson Elliott—"

"Stop interrupting me, please. I find it rude and annoying," Madison snapped. "Now, Mr. Elliott—"

"But all of my good friends just call me Steve," he persisted.

Madison regarded the broad smile housed in a mouth that was sumptuous and boyish at the same time. She tried to force an expression of aggravation onto her face, but realized that she had already begun to enjoy the game of cat and mouse they were playing more than she should. There was an air about him that was both irresistible and engaging, yet she was not about to let such a pompous foreigner in on the fact that he'd moved her.

"Mr. Elliott, while I would love to stand around trading

witty commentary with a presumptuous stranger, frankly, I've got better things to do with my time."

Madison turned away from him in an attempt to keep her eyes from betraying the lie she'd just told him. At that moment there was nothing she'd rather do than remain in his presence, but she was a woman who was pursued, not the other way around. She walked away from Stevenson Elliott, certain that his eyes were trained on her receding figure as she felt them boring into her back. The natural twist of her huggable hips as she walked was slightly exaggerated for his benefit and his torment.

Stevenson laughed out loud, taken by the beauty with the unconventional hairstyle and prickly tongue. He watched her as she crossed the room with a self-assured spring in her step that was admirable. He started to go after her, but instinctively knew that it was probably not a good idea. This silver-clad goddess was hell on wheels, of that he was certain, and a distraction like her was the last thing he needed in his life. There were expectations on his shoulders that required clear thinking and undistracted diligence. Yet even as he reminded himself of his obligations, his smoldering eyes followed her around the room.

"There you guys are," Madison said as she came upon the table where her parents were seated.

Dr. and Mrs. Joseph Daniels were sharing a table with Judge Kelly from the southern district of New York, his wife, Patricia, Senator Houssman from Poughkeepsie and his wife, Carla, and Georgetta Price, a world-renowned Broadway diva.

Joseph rose to greet his daughter, his facing beaming with pride.

"You made it, pumpkin," he said, kissing her cheek. Joseph Daniels's eyes lit up at the sight of his youngest child. His warm-brown face gave way to a wide smile, tiny laugh lines appearing in the corners of his eyes. Anyone who knew him knew that he had a heart as good as gold and as soft as putty when it came to his two daughters. Despite the trials and tribulations that Madison had dragged them through over the years, and mountains of worries finally pushed aside, there was nothing that could diminish his love and adoration for her, his youngest daughter.

Elmira tilted her face upward slightly to receive her daughter's peck on her cheek.

"Everyone, you remember my baby girl, Madison?" Joseph asked with pride.

"Joe, I don't think you can call this beautiful young woman your baby girl anymore. She's all grown up!" Senator Houssman said.

"She certainly is. Why, the last time we saw you, young lady, it was with a face full of braces and pretty little pigtails," Patricia Houssman chimed. "You, my dear, are an absolute knockout."

"Thank you, Mrs. Houssman. Senator." Madison smiled.

Joseph pulled out the chair to his left for Madison, who slid into the seat with a radiant smile.

"I don't care how old or beautiful a woman she becomes—she will always be my baby girl!" Joseph said proudly, squeezing Madison's shoulders firmly before taking his seat again.

Chatting resumed at the table as the band played and the champagne flowed. Thus, the evening progressed. It was one of the first political affairs that Madison had attended where she actually was not bored out of her mind. Georgetta Price was a laugh a minute, regaling their table with stories of the many schizophrenic directors and unscrupulous starlets she'd come across in her career, which spanned more than three decades. Madison listened with half an ear, as her mind remained preoccupied with thoughts of the charismatic young man with the English tongue and charming wit. Her feminine senses had been stroked by his teasing, making it difficult to forget him. She surreptitiously scanned the room from time to time, hoping to catch a glimpse of him; however, like Cinderella at the ball, he seemed to have vanished into thin air.

As the evening wore on, Madison made every effort to push all thoughts of the handsome stranger from her mind, reminding herself that she did not need romantic entanglements in her life right now. She was doing well all by herself and the last thing she needed was for some guy to come along and make her lose her focus. Despite occasional pangs of loneliness that were normal for a young woman, she rather enjoyed the time and space of living alone in the city that never sleeps.

It had only been six short months since she'd moved off of her bourgeois parents' luxurious Southern estate and out of their reach. Leaving the drama and scandal she had caused in North Carolina behind her, she had seized the opportunity for a fresh start in the Big Apple. New York City was a metropolis of big buildings and even bigger dreams, and unlike the glove in the infamous O. J. Simpson trial, it was a perfect fit. Gone was the flowing warm brown hair that had not been cut more than a quarter of an inch since she was five years old and in its place were short, funky new locks in hair that had been dyed honey-blond. This new hairstyle was becoming, giving her buttermilk complexion a fresh, quirky look.

Since she'd landed in New York, Madison had become devoted to living a healthy lifestyle by eating right and working out three times a week at the New York Sports Club. Her naturally sexy, curvaceous frame was in tip-top form physically, which also boosted her mental and emotional states. She had never felt more motivated and ready to take charge of her destiny. Of course, she had yet to figure out what that destiny was, leaving her reliant on the monthly allowance her father sent. Her Upper East Side apartment was small, yet chicly decorated, and by subsidizing what her father gave her with work at odd jobs—ranging from dog walker to yoga instructor—she was able to live a comfortable lifestyle.

Money matters didn't concern her, however, because she realized that she was a work in progress who had come a long way from where she once was. She was contemplating her options and even considering going back to college on a part-time basis. Admittedly, she was enjoying the relative calm of a life that did not include nightly partying, alcoholic binges and the distraction of juggling relationships like a circus trickster. That was precisely why she'd sworn off sordid affairs with men…handsome, charming men.

"How's everyone enjoying the party?"

Madison started at the sound of that baritone voice, instantly recognizable. She felt a sudden flush in her cheeks when his strong hand landed lightly on her shoulder. She suppressed her body's urge to tremble under his unexpected touch.

"We're enjoying it just fine, young man. Say, aren't you Gregory Elliott's son?" Senator Houssman asked.

"Yes, sir, I'm Stevenson Elliott. It's a pleasure to meet you, Senator Houssman."

"Your father and I did some business together years ago when I was a consultant in the natural resources industry. I lived in England for over three years. Very fine man, that Gregory Elliott. Is he here tonight, son? I'd love to say hello," the senator remarked earnestly.

"Yes, sir. He and my mother are seated right over there, with Congressman Powers."

"Oh, yes. Excuse me, folks," the senator said, rising and shaking Steve's hand before departing.

Steve walked around the table, shaking hands with the men at the table and delivering compliments to the ladies who were seated there.

"Stevenson, this is our daughter, Madison. Darling, say hello," Elmira said, her voice a tad too cheery for Madison's tastes.

"Mother, we met earlier in the evening," Madison answered dryly, avoiding making eye contact with Steve.

She picked up the glass in front of her, taking a long sip of the cool, sparkling water to soothe the sudden dryness that had developed in her throat.

"Yes, we have. In fact, that's precisely why I came over to your table. I was standing across the room wondering to myself if the lovely young lady would like to join me on the dance floor. I think we'd be a perfect match to show the more mature folks how to get this party started the right way," Steve said.

Madison looked up at him finally, glancing from his extended hand to his face. A flash of benign irritation passed through her eyes as she stared at him without speaking. She ran her tongue over her bottom lip as she thought of a tactful way to get him to leave her alone, but when his gaze fell to her mouth and he smiled seductively, she realized how suggestively her action might have been perceived.

"What a lovely idea. Go on, Madison," Elmira encouraged, her lips spread as wide as they could possibly go without splitting her face in half.

Madison gave a slight smile, quickly putting in check the old Madison, who would have snapped her mother's head off right in front of a roomful of people for her transparent attempt at interfering in her life and matchmaking. She took Steve's hand and rose from her chair, allowing him to lead her out into the middle of the dance floor. The band began to play "So Amazing" by the late Luther Vandross just as Steve slid his right arm around Madison's body, drawing her to him closely as if they had danced together a thousand times before. Madison rested the palm of her left hand on his shoulder blade, while he closed her right hand in his. His long fingers wrapped around hers tightly. In her heels she was still three or four inches shorter than him, landing the top of her forehead against his chin. A perfect fit.

"So, Madison Daniels. Pretty name for a pretty woman," he said.

Their faces were just inches apart. Madison could feel the warmth of his breath on her nose and it made her conscious of how close their bodies were to one another, but at the same time rendered her incapable of breaking the intimacy even if she wanted to. It felt too good to sever.

"Thank you," she said, all too aware of the erratic beat of her heart.

"No, thank you…for sparing a few moments of your precious time to dance with me," Steve said, his voice tinged with mocking amusement.

"So, let me guess. You're some sort of funny guy, huh?" Madison inquired. "Or so you think."

"No, not at all. Actually, I'm usually quite serious. Some people might say that I'm extremely intense. It must be something about the romantic lighting and the festive mood in this room that has me reacting like this. Or it could just be the company I'm keeping."

The seductive lilt to his voice was making her feel warm and causing her to be all too aware of the sensations his body against hers was creating.

"So, Mr. Elliott, when you aren't acting out of character, what do you do?" Madison asked, attempting to steer the conversation to an area that would not cause her temperature to continue to climb.

"Well, I'm a citizen of Great Britain and back home I work with my father."

"And what does your father do?"

"He is Chairman and CEO of the Elliott Corporation. Our business is manufacturing. But I don't want to bore you with shop talk when I'd much rather talk about you and how striking you are."

"I see. Well, Mr. Elliott, you're a long ways away from Great Britain, in case you didn't notice. I'm not sure how things are done there, but here in America, we don't fixate on a person's exterior because we are astute enough to realize that what lies beyond that shell, the interior, is where the treasure actually rests."

Steve stepped away from Madison, extending his arm and spinning her around. His eyes remained trained on hers as he pulled her into his arms again.

"I noticed that I'm not in England." He smiled. "But thank you for your tip. I'll definitely take it to heart."

The undertone of his comment was not lost on Madison and once again, her pulse raced.

"My parents and I are here on a vacation of sorts. We had some business in California and my mother has a dear friend who is a native New Yorker, so she convinced my father to spend a few days in the city after our business concluded. My mother's friend, Mrs. Andrews, the widow of Congressman Andrews, invited us as her guests to tonight's affair. We're scheduled to return home in a few days."

"Oh," Madison said and was immediately embarrassed by the sound of disappointment in her tone.

"Now it's your turn, Ms. Daniels. Your dad is a doctor, yes?"

"Yes, he is. He's a cosmetic surgeon. My mom is a professional housewife and busybody. We're from Charlotte, North Carolina. Ever been south?"

"Yes, I've been to Florida a couple of times."

"Let me guess…West Palm Beach, right? I'm not talking about the touristy south. Have you ever been to the *South?* General stores, wraparound porches and sugarcane fields?"

Steve grew silent for a moment, a cloud passing over his face. Madison studied him, poising her lips to ask what was wrong. Just as quickly as it landed, however, the cloud was gone and his smile returned.

"Aah, the *South*. No, can't say that I have had the pleasure. Maybe someday you will volunteer to be my tour guide to your South when you don't have anything better to do with your time."

"Your insolence continues to astound me, Mr. Elliott," Madison laughed.

"I'm just a believer in the power of positive thinking, Ms. Daniels," he said.

"Really? Well, unfortunately for you, I live here in Manhattan now."

"That's okay. I haven't seen much of New York, either, since I've been here, so maybe you could show me around your new home."

Steve's last words were more of a statement than a request. He smiled that infectious smile again, warding off any attack that Madison might be inclined to make because of his presumptuous declaration. Her lips trembled as she smiled back at him, their eyes locked. It was a charged moment in which no words were necessary or available from either of them. The pounding of their heartbeats was noise enough.

In an attempt to quiet the fluttering sensation in her stomach and the throbbing in her temples, Madison rested her head against his shoulder and they silently continued to move across the floor. Several other couples had followed their lead, taking to the dance floor to move to the sound of the band. Yet, Steve and Madison failed to notice anyone else around them as they moved against one another, each getting to know and appreciate the feel and

"Hey, what's going on here? Get that thing out of her face."

"So, Madison, does Edward Worthington know that you've taken up with Stevenson Elliott, son of the billionaire Gregory Elliott? Isn't he a little young for your tastes?" the reporter persisted, her mouth twisted into a nasty sneer.

The light from the camera pointed at her by the cameraman was bright, illuminating her and the bewildered Steve. The scene quickly drew the attention of the entire room of well-appointed people.

"What are you talking about? I'm not in contact with Edward Worthington and I don't know anything about him and his wife," Madison stammered.

The reporter was poised to ask another question when, with the same swiftness as the woman and her crew had descended, security approached what had now turned into a melee of sorts. The band had stopped playing and every eye in the room was trained on the center of the dance floor. Steve roughly shoved the microphone away from Madison, causing the reporter to stumble backward, nearly losing her balance. The cameraman moved in, lowering his camera to his side, and Steve challenged him to make a move. The reporter stayed her guy with a hand on his arm, while Steve's fist remained tightly balled at his side. He draped an arm protectively around the speechless Madison, and as security harshly removed the reporter and the two cameramen, Steve began moving her away from the action.

Joseph Daniels approached, yelling at either the security guards or the reporters or both; it was unclear. He followed the group out into the lobby area, his outrage at the press' insinuation into his daughter's privacy apparent. Steve kept his arm around Madison and was steering her in the opposite direction of security, the press and her father when his own parents intercepted them.

"Stevenson, it's time for us to leave," Gregory Elliott said sternly, approaching from behind them.

Steve whirled around. "Dad, I—"

"Now, Stevenson."

Gregory Elliott was a couple of inches shorter than his son, his portly belly and balding head of graying hair indicative of his approach to middle age. Yet he had a power and a commanding nature that not many people would dare to defy.

"Dad, I'd like you to meet Madison Daniels," Steve insisted, looking his father squarely in the face.

Reluctantly, Gregory pulled his gaze from his son, turning toward Madison for the first time. His eyes bored into her, taking her in from head to toe and back to head again.

"Ms. Daniels," he said, by way of a greeting, his head nodding slightly.

"Mom, this is Madison," Steve said, turning to his mother, who had just joined their circle.

"Young lady," Janice Elliott said with her face set in a hard mask.

The ensuing chill in the air was noticeable, although the room itself was quite warm. Madison, who was slowly coming back to herself after the shock of the confrontation with the press, found her tongue again.

"Mr. and Mrs. Elliott, it is my pleasure meeting you."

She did not wait for a response, but merely turned to focus her attention on Steve. "Steve, thank you for your help. It was very nice meeting you as well. Take care."

With that she spun in a half circle, stepping out of Steve's embrace. She moved quickly away from the trio, her head high and a no-nonsense swagger in her hips. She heard Steve call after her, although she pretended not to. Outside the ballroom, Madison encountered her father with the hall's manager, who was apologizing profusely for his security having allowed the press to sneak into the affair. It turned out that the individuals were from one of the sleazy gossip rags and had managed to create a diversion outside to enable them to slip past the security guard when he was pulled away from the door.

"Dad, I'm going home," Madison said as he approached, his face distorted with concern.

"Maddie, are you all right, dear?"

"Yes, Dad, I'm fine. I'm just going to go home and forget about this night," Madison sighed.

"Why don't I drive you home? I'll have the valet get the rental and—"

"No, no, Dad. It's okay. I'll catch a taxi. You should get back in there with Mother. You know how she gets. I'll stop by the hotel to see you guys Sunday afternoon before you leave, okay?"

Madison kissed her father brusquely on the cheek and moved past him, before he could protest.

Upon losing sight of Madison's quickly retreating frame, Steve turned on his parents. "That was disgraceful. How could you guys be so rude to her—as if she'd done something to you?"

"No, son, what's disgraceful is the scene this young lady just caused and, furthermore, pulled you into. How utterly embarrassing!" Gregory stormed.

"You don't even know what happened," Steve protested.

"We heard enough. Unless you're going to tell me there's been some sort of mistaken identity, that reporter indicated that that young lady has been caught up in some sort of sordid sex scandal. Judging from the overexposed manner in which she was dressed, I can't say that I'm the least bit surprised. Now let's go home."

"I'll catch up with you guys later," Steve said.

With that he walked abruptly across the floor, very aware that his father had taken a few steps after him before his mother stopped him by squeezing his forearm.

Once on the street, the valet hailed a yellow taxi and within minutes of her departure from the hotel, Madison was safely ensconced in the backseat of the sedan. There was a line of departing cars ahead of them, all waiting to make their exit out onto the busy Manhattan street. She closed her eyes and ears to block out the cacophony of the world that existed outside her cab, tilting her head back against the seat as she willed the tension from her body. How long she would have to pay for the mistakes of her past she didn't know. But what she did know was that she was tired of people looking at her as if she were damaged goods.

Her thoughts immediately traveled to Stevenson Elliott. He was one smooth operator, and there was a time in the not too distant past when she would have matched his charm and wit, tit for tat, and enjoyed every moment of it. Yet Madison realized that if she was serious about propelling her life into a direction that was far removed and decidedly different from the one it had been headed in, she could not jump to attention at the sight of every charming and good-looking man she met. Once upon a time, discretion had not been a word with which she maintained any level of familiarity, and this lack had cost her more than it had gained. If there was ever any hope of being seen for the person she truly was inside, she needed to lead a personal life that did not alert the media bloodhounds that seemed to be attracted to her like flies to cow manure.

A sudden sharp rap against the back window startled Madison. She sat upright in her seat, her eyes popping open. At first glance, all she could see was the black tuxedo jacket of a man, as the cab had resumed inching its way down the driveway toward the street. Suddenly, the body outside the taxi lowered itself and she was astonished to find the handsome face of the man she had just been willing herself not to think about smiling through the glass at her. She blinked, looked at him with a dumbfounded expression, yet made no other movement. He rapped on the window again, and then wiggled two fingers in an up-and-down motion, indicating that he wanted her to bring down the glass that separated them.

"Yes?" she asked as she pressed the lever just long enough to allow for a two-inch crack through which warm spring air brushed her forehead.

"I was wondering if we could share a cab. It's quite busy out here," Steve said.

"Share a cab to where?" she asked sardonically, her eyebrows a knot of genuine confusion.

"Well, I could have the driver drop you off first and then take me to my destination. Won't you open the door or are you going to leave a poor stranded foreigner out in the cold?"

He smiled that scorching smile again, the one that could

melt a frozen block of dry ice in zero-point-two seconds flat and leave it sizzling like bacon over an open flame.

"First of all," she replied slowly, "it's not the least bit cold out there."

Steve's mouth turned into a boyish pout, and that look was twice as deadly as his smile. Madison could not stop the laughter that bubbled up from her stomach and spilled from her lips. She clicked the lock and slid to her left to allow room.

"Boy, are all American woman as immovable as you?" Steve asked once he was securely inside the vehicle.

"Don't start or you'll be bounced back out of this taxi and onto the pavement so fast that your visitor's visa will feel the shock!" Madison warned.

Steve held up two fingers in the peace sign, beaming warmly at her.

"I find it amazing that for such a little thing, you move very fast! I ran out after you and barely caught a glimpse of those beautiful legs as you slid into the taxi. Another five seconds and I would have missed you completely."

"Steve, what do you want from me?" Madison asked.

The old Madison would have had something twice as coy and cultured to say, but at this point, as engaging as this tall, dark and handsome man was, she was not in the mood. After the outrage of her encounter with the press, the cold shoulder she'd received from Mr. and Mrs. Elliott and the enraged outburst of her father, she'd had enough for one night. She was tired and annoyed.

"Why do you automatically assume that I want something from you?"

"That's because most men do want something, especially the wild ones who chase women out into the street."

"Touché. Okay, I do want something from you. I'd like an hour of your company—just one hour to be spent over coffee perhaps. I'd like to talk to you and listen to you and have a mere sixty minutes more of the pleasure I find in being in your presence."

Just when Madison had believed that at the age of twenty-five she had heard every line from every guy, had memorized the instruction manual of the quintessential player trying to play her and could never again be caught off guard by anything, Stevenson Elliott entered her taxi and threw her completely off balance. This was especially true because of the fact that somehow she instinctively knew that the words he had just spoken were authentic and not just those of a smooth-talking Mac dropping sweet lines to hook some fresh catch.

## Chapter 3

Sixty minutes turned into six hours. Those six hours were spent at a tall, round table for two, tucked in a back corner of a twenty-four-hour café sipping lattes and picking at powdered, sugar-frosted scones. Their conversation was slow and easy, straying from random subjects with the agility that usually came with time but had somehow been mastered by them instantaneously. Madison found Steve surprisingly candid, as he talked about his family and childhood. In addition, he was also as keen to listen to her speak as he was to talk himself, and she got the impression that he was genuinely interested in hearing her speak as opposed to simply trying to earn brownie points.

"I've been to England a few times myself...with my family. We visited London, of course, Buckinghamshire and Oxford. When my sister Kennedy was in high school she even entertained the idea of applying to the university there. I was struck by the beauty of the country, but I could never imagine living there. I mean, it was rainy most of the time we were there and the temperatures pretty much stayed the same all of the time. Have you ever thought about living somewhere else?" Madison inquired.

"Well, it's not all that bad. I mean, it's got a mixture of different types of people, great beautiful natural sights and besides, we've got two awesome football teams. I mean, it's no New York City, but it's nice."

"I'm sorry, Steve. I didn't mean to trash your homeland. I was just wondering aloud. I tend to open my mouth wide and stick my foot in it sometimes before I realize what I'm saying or to whom I'm saying it."

"No, please don't apologize. To answer your question, I have thought about living somewhere else. You see, I was not actually born in England."

"Oh, no?" Madison asked, raising her eyebrows in surprise.

Steve's clipped British accent was as authentic as any she'd ever heard. Secretly, the lilt of his words and the velvet cadence of his voice had already begun to do something to her. She found it hard to believe that he'd ever spoken any other language or dialect, so perfect was his intonation of the king's language.

"No. I was born in the West Indies—St. Elizabeth, Jamaica, to be exact," he confessed.

"I would never have guessed that," Madison responded. "Do you visit home often?"

A noticeable shift in Steve's relaxed features occurred and his eyes filled with something she could not discern, but could not deny existed. "Well, no, I haven't been to Jamaica since I was five years old. It's a long story, but once my parents made England our home, we pretty much left our earlier lives behind."

Madison regarded Steve quietly, taking a long sip from her coffee. Though she'd only known him for a matter of hours, she could tell that the thing that cast a shadow over his words as he spoke about his birthplace was a profound sense of loss. As she didn't know him well enough to push for more, she just reached across the table and placed her hand over the one of his that had absently begun drumming on the table.

"I know a little something about leaving the past behind. Sometimes that's what you have to do in order to make way for a better future," she said softly.

Their eyes met and held, and the flurry of emotions between them was combustible. Madison's butter-pecan cheeks flamed, bringing color to her face and a glisten to her eyes.

"Someday you'll have to tell me what that whole thing with the reporters was about," he said at long last.

"Steve—" Madison began to protest.

Steve shook his head vehemently, cutting her off.

"I didn't say today...someday, perhaps. Someday when you've grown to know me and to trust me with all of you," he interrupted.

"What makes you so sure we're headed toward that day?" Madison asked.

"I believe in fate, Madison. I do not believe that there are accidental meetings or chance phenomena. People come into your life for a reason. You are confronted with various situations for a purpose. Sometimes, we choose to ignore those signs…maybe because we're afraid or because we believe that what we've planned for ourselves is the only avenue that we should travel. However, I've learned to accept what is presented to me, knowing that God would not put anything before me that is not meant for me to have."

"Are you a religious man?" Madison asked.

"I like to think that I'm in touch with my spiritual self. When I was little, my parents and I attended Mass every Sunday bright and early. I took communion, listened to the word of God and did all the things a good little Catholic boy was supposed to do. Yet, I don't think it was until college that I really began to understand what I'd been reading and hearing all of my life. Now I don't go to church much, but I know that there is one ruler, one entity whose mercy directs all things great and small. I also know that the responsibility lies within me to live a good life and follow my purpose. What about you? Are you a good little church girl?"

"Me? Well, like you, I was raised going to church. Say your prayers, repent for your sins and honor your parents. I don't think I ever really felt a connection to God though. I mean, believing in something is one thing but trusting in it to govern your life is something entirely different."

Steve placed his other hand over Madison's, smiling at her. "You have a hard time with trusting, don't you?"

"What makes you say that?" Madison asked defensively.

They held each other's gaze for a moment before they both erupted into side-splitting laughter.

"All right, so you might be right. But, in my defense,

there are a lot of people out in the world who don't mean you any good. You can't trust everybody you come across. For all I know, you could be a mass murderer, wanted all across England for accosting women in taxis and dismembering them," Madison laughed.

"For that matter, so could you. In fact, I do think I've seen a Wanted poster with a woman who bore a striking resemblance to you. Let me get a good look at you."

Steve leaned closer, his chest resting against the edge of the round table that separated them. "Mmm-hmm—a perfect match."

"What am I wanted for?"

"The charge was breaking hearts in the first degree. I think I'm going to make a phone call to see if they're still offering a reward for your capture," he said.

"Oh, like you need reward money. The Elliott Corporation is one of the highest-grossing corporations in this century," she said.

"So, what does that mean?"

"That means you're loaded. Oh, I'm sorry, was that supposed to be a secret?"

"Let me correct you—my dad is loaded. The Elliott Corporation is his baby, not mine. Yes, I work for him, and yes, he'd like me to take over the business one day. To tell you the truth, I'm not sure if that's what I want."

"I see. Well, feel free to correct me again if I'm wrong, but your dad doesn't seem like the type of man who's going to let his son go off and *find himself* as opposed to taking his place at the helm of the family business. Just an observation," she said.

Steve smiled a half smile and leaned back in his chair.

"You're not wrong, but I guess we'll just wait and see what happens, huh?"

As the sun began to come up on the horizon, lighting up the never-sleeping, but quieter than normal streets of Manhattan, Steve insisted on sharing Madison's taxi uptown to her apartment on East Seventy-fourth Street. They sat shoulder to shoulder, quietly enjoying the short ride. When they arrived, Steve paid the driver to wait while he walked Madison to the building's door.

"I'd like to see you again," he said softly.

They were facing each other, the fingers of their hands locked together. Once again, Madison's faced felt flushed as she looked up into warm brown eyes. "When are you leaving town?"

"In a few days. Can I see you tonight?"

The urgency in his voice mirrored the feeling that had come over her. She struggled to recapture the common sense that had seemed to escape her mind from the moment she'd met Stevenson Elliott, but it was no use. She was under a spell and breaking it simply was not in her power at this point.

"Tonight?" She echoed his words as she stalled for time to get her mouth to say what the nagging voice in the back of her mind was telling her to say.

"Yes, tonight. You call the shots. Anytime you say. Anywhere you say. I just want to see you again," Steve said forcefully.

The earnestness in his voice caused her resolve to melt instantly and the voice of doubt was bound, gagged and shoved in the back of a closet.

"Eight o'clock?" she asked.

"Eight o'clock. I'll be here to pick you up."

Steve seemed relieved as he accepted her concession to his request. He searched her face, as if wanting to memorize every inch of it in case he never had the opportunity to see her again.

"I'll see you tonight," Madison said, reassuring him.

Steve leaned forward, grazing his lips ever so lightly across Madison's left cheek, and walked away. Her hand rose, her fingers landing on the spot he'd kissed, which was warm and tingling.

# Chapter 4

Madison tossed an olive-colored blouse across the bed, changing her mind for the eighth time in the past hour. After spending all night with Steve, Madison had come back to her apartment, showered and lain across her bed. Unable to sleep, however, she'd gotten up after an hour, donned her workout gear and walked the three blocks to the gym where she worked out daily and taught yoga classes. All through the vigorous workout she undertook, her mind replayed the previous night. She could not believe that one chance meeting had upset the balance of her life so much. Steve Elliott had left an indelible mark on her, which was not an easy feat.

She decided to stop thinking about what had happened and pondering the implications of it. After spending hours contemplating the impact that this man had had on her, she concluded that all she needed to do was to live in the moment and enjoy herself. It was not exactly as if this was a foreign concept for her, for Madison had lived her entire adult life following this approach. However, in the months since she'd relocated to New York City, she'd purposely shed her former attitude and now allowed reason and consideration of all angles to guide her. She didn't want to be known as the fly-by-the-seat-of-her-pants woman she'd been known as. Yet she also knew that unlike many of her past escapades, passing some time with Steve would not prove detrimental to her. Steve was a good guy with whom she'd crossed paths and shared a connection unlike any other she'd ever experienced. Why not take pleasure in it for as long as it lasted?

With that thought in mind, she settled on an orange miniskirt and an ivory halter top patterned with thin pink and orange stripes. After a hot bath, she freshened up a three-day-old pedicure and curled up on the sofa with a magazine. She turned page after page, unable to focus on the fashions before her because of a severe case of distraction. Steve's face kept flashing before her eyes, his sexy smile and seductive voice running freely through her imagination. She chided herself for allowing her mind to run away with her senses over a guy she'd just met, but there was something so alluringly different about Steve that she could not help herself. She dozed and found that visions of him ran through her dreams. By the time he arrived to pick her up for their date, she was filled with a heady excitement that carried her on air down the stairs.

"What would you like to do tonight?" Steve asked as he held open the passenger door of a rented Mercedes.

"I don't know. It's such a beautiful night…let's do

something outdoors. Oh, I know. We can drive down to the South Street Seaport. There's always something going on down there," Madison answered excitedly.

"South Street Seaport it is. You're going to have to direct me though."

Madison settled into the soft leather seat and they meandered through city traffic. Their conversation and laughter flowed like syrup over a stack of hot pancakes, their words sticking in all the right places. Steve parked on the corner of Fulton Street and they walked slowly toward Pier Seventeen on South Street, the cool breeze, coming from the direction of the water, caressing their faces.

"So, Madison Daniels, you've never told me what a country girl such as yourself is doing here in the big city, all alone and on your own. Don't tell me it's that same sad cliché?"

"Which one is that?"

"The one about the girl who came here chasing some guy, found out he was a cross-dresser and it didn't work out," Steve laughed.

Madison dipped a celery stick into the bowl of blue cheese dressing that had come with her order of buffalo wings. They were seated at Uno's, one of the cafes located on the upstairs outer deck of the food court, a view of the water and small dinner boats to their left. The lights of the shops and boats along the water sparkled more brilliantly tonight, it seemed, although the real illumination that engulfed them had nothing to do with the scenery.

"Ha!" Madison exploded. "Do you honestly think that I'd ever chase a guy somewhere? Hmph, I guess you've got a lot to learn about me, Mr. Elliott."

"Nah, I was just teasing. I know that you are the *pursuee,* not the *pursuer.* You enjoy having men crumble at your feet while you look down upon them, laugh and then grind your stilettos into their tortured hearts."

Steve leaned forward and wiped a spot of blue cheese from the corner of Madison's mouth. His touch was so gentle that for a moment she lost all train of thought.

"I think you watch too many movies. I'm not at all the femme fatale you're making me out to be. But to answer your question, no, I didn't come to New York chasing anyone. I guess you could say I was looking for someone."

"Who?"

Madison studied the lights shimmering on the water for a moment before returning her gaze to Steve's face. She didn't know why she was talking so much to someone that twenty-four hours ago she hadn't even known existed. She was not a talker, not by a long shot, but maybe she had been waiting all of her life for the right person to talk to.

"Me," she said at last.

Steve nodded his head slowly, understanding registering on his handsome face as if he, too, had been waiting for the right person to talk to about the things that were going on inside him. At that moment the connection between the two of them was undeniable and, furthermore, neither of them wanted to even try to pretend that something unexpected yet amazing had not occurred in their meeting.

Steve reached out and stayed the hand that Madison was using to feed another piece of celery into her mouth. He leaned forward and when his lips found hers, her breath caught in her throat. Soft pliable lips pressed against hers with a tenderness that was so marked that it was more passionate than even the most ardent and lustful kiss she'd ever shared with anyone. He withdrew slowly, his smile that of a bashful adolescent. From that moment on, they both knew that they had innocently stumbled upon a situation that neither would be able to walk away from unchanged.

## Chapter 5

"Stevenson, what do you mean you are not ready to go home? You know your father has a lot on his plate right now with the expansion. He's already spent more time in the States than he could afford to take, just to indulge our pleas for a family holiday."

"I know that, Mother, but that doesn't have anything to do with me," Steve answered.

"Nothing to do with you? Nothing to do… Correct me if I'm wrong, son, but don't you work for your father? Of course it has everything to do with you." Janice Elliott huffed as she considered her son's serious countenance and his earnest request. She resealed the designer duffel bag that she had just closed for the second time as she stuffed yet another toiletry in the already full carrier. They'd bought two extra pieces of luggage in order to accommodate her shopping expenditures, and she feared that she would still not have enough room. She'd been considering the possibility that she'd have to have the hotel ship some of her belongings when Steve had knocked at their Waldorf Astoria suite door.

Another look at her son and Janice realized that this conversation would require her complete attention. Their flight to London was scheduled for an eight o'clock departure the next morning and she had already done most of the packing for herself and her husband, who was in the bedroom of their suite at the posh hotel taking a conference call. Janice stopped her packing, sighed and sat down on the edge of an ottoman.

"I didn't mean it that way. I just meant that… Well, you and I both know that Dad can handle things for the time being without me," Steve said at length.

He moved across the room and sat down on the sofa. Janice eyed her son, her only child, marveling at the fine young man he'd become, which was a behavior she'd found herself engaging in more and more often recently. He was slightly taller than his father, having inherited her side of the family's stature. His chestnut-brown skin matched Gregory's, and he shared the same powerful features. She watched as her son matched the tips of his long fingers together, pressing each hand against the other, something he always did when he was thinking or pressed by some urgent decision. Janice's brow wrinkled as she realized that her son had something very important on his mind. She moved closer to him, taking a seat beside him on the sofa.

"What's going on, Stevenson?" she asked.

"There's nothing going on, Mother. I just want to spend some more time here in the States. Look, I know that Dad's got a lot going on and I understand why you guys need to get back right away. But, Mother, I've been working day in and day out since I finished at the university. I need a little break."

"Isn't this a little sudden, son? I mean, you haven't mentioned anything about wanting to take some time off before. Why now?" Janice pressed, wanting her son to confide in her the way he used to.

"There's no specific reason. We're here in New York City and it's a great city. I just thought I could take a few more days…perhaps a week or two to get to see more of it. Take in some shows, a couple of basketball games at the Garden…you know. Look, I'll be back at home and at work before Dad even misses me. Come on, Mother, what do you say?"

"Well, Stevenson, you're a grown man. You certainly don't need my permission," Janice replied.

"I know that, Mother, but I want it just the same."

"No, what you want is for me to soften the request to your father," Janice countered.

She knew her son well and she also knew that like her, he was well aware of his father's demanding nature.

"All right. I was thinking that Dad would be less likely to flip out if you were on my side," Steve admitted. "You know that you have a way with him. So what do you say?" Steve said, nudging his mother's thigh with his leg.

Janice grinned as she looked into her son's face, never having been able to resist that infectious Elliott smile of either her child or his father. She'd gladly take the brunt of Gregory's discord if it meant sparing Stevenson the same.

"Oh, all right," she said. "But you'll have to make your own arrangements. We're not paying for you to keep your suite here. It's an expense that isn't necessary, considering the amount of time you've actually spent indoors. Where will you stay?"

"That's already taken care of. I got a room at the Crowne Plaza near the United Nations building. It's right here in the heart of Midtown and it's a whole lot cheaper than this place."

"Oh, you have?" Janice said, eyeing her son suspiciously. "Well, I guess you've thought this all through. All right, well, make sure you contact the travel agent, Elaine, and have her reissue your return flight ticket. And when exactly will that be?"

"I'll call you in a few days, Mother, and let you know. Listen, you and Dad have a safe trip and I'll talk to you soon," Steve said, kissing his mother swiftly on the cheek before jumping up from the sofa.

"Aren't you going to wait to speak with your father?" Janice called as he began making his way toward the door.

"Oh, you know he's going to be on the phone with those Wesco guys for at least another hour. I've got to get going…I have plans for tonight. Don't worry, I've already packed my belongings. You can just have the bellhop leave my bags with the concierge and I'll pick them up tomorrow. Love you, Mother," Steve said.

With that, he was gone, leaving a puzzled Janice staring after the closed door of the hotel suite, wondering just what had gotten into her son. She also wondered exactly what he meant by a cheaper hotel, hoping that he hadn't checked in to some economy dive.

She slipped into a reverie of a time that didn't seem so

far away. When she was her son's age, her life had been difficult at best. She and Gregory struggled to make ends meet while getting his business off the ground. Janice remembered the early days vividly. She'd given birth to her only child when she and Gregory still lived in a tiny two-room flat that lacked indoor plumbing in the rural farmlands of Jamaica. Both she and Gregory had been raised in the countryside of St. Elizabeth. Gregory was a couple of years older than her, but their families had attended the same ramshackle church where they'd played together as children. Both she and her sister Claudia had carried crushes on Gregory Elliott all through grade school, but it was Janice who'd won his heart.

Janice always knew that Gregory would be successful. She would sit and listen to him talk for hours about how he was going to get out of the country, out of Jamaica and live a good life. As the youngest of five children in a Seventh Day Adventist family led by a hardworking but indebted farming couple, Gregory had dreamed of a life far removed from the one he'd known. He was sorely embarrassed by his family's lack, even though all of their neighbors, and the entire town for that matter, were no better off. Gregory became an exceptional student and a determined young man. He had done whatever was necessary to become the success he always knew he could be, and she'd supported him in every way she knew how. Janice supported him emotionally and physically as he earned, bribed and brown-nosed his way into a successful career after starting out in the natural resources manufacturing and trade business in Jamaica.

By the time Steve turned five years old, Gregory had relocated to England and brought his family over after a six-month separation, leaving the poverty behind. In doing so, they'd also gladly severed all ties to their shameful beginnings. Gregory made every one of his and Janice's dreams come true, and she was proud to know that their son would have options and opportunities that they had only dreamed of when they were his age. She'd always reasoned that someday there would be retribution for the things they'd done, but she never let that certainty deter her. One of her greatest joys was the knowledge that her son would never have to work as hard as his father had worked. He would never have to sacrifice the way they'd had to. Most importantly to her, his conscience would never be burdened by sins of the past the way hers was. As heir to the Elliott Corporation, one of the largest import/export companies in England, Stevenson was assured of his future.

Janice smiled again as she thought of her son. She realized that he did deserve a little time off, as he had always worked hard and lived up to every expectation they held for him, even when he was just a little boy. Soon enough it would be time for him to take over more of his father's operations and settle down to begin a family of his own. She looked forward to the day when she and Gregory could sit back and enjoy the fruits of their labors. She'd already begun planning the trips abroad she'd wanted to take and the extended excursions she'd always dreamed of. Janice could not imagine having a more perfect life and had no doubts that it would continue to just get sweeter.

# Chapter 6

"This place reminds me of the nightclubs back home in England," Steve shouted over the loud, pulsing house music that boomed from every corner of the dimly lit room.

They were on the upper floor of Webster Hall, a trendy dance club located on the Lower East Side of Manhattan. It was housed inside an old warehouse on one of the lower-numbered streets in a diverse neighborhood. The cavernous club contained room after room of eclectic décor and varying musical stylings.

"This is only my second time coming here, and I still can't get enough. You've got every type of person in here from rocker to hip-hop heads and everything in between. It's wild," Madison shouted back over the din of the music and voices.

They'd spent the past few days around the city. Steve

professed that he wanted to see every inch of New York City and, despite the fact that Madison was a recent transplant herself, he appointed her his personal tour guide. They'd gone to the Empire State Building in midtown Manhattan, Flushing Meadow Park in Queens and various other points of interest in and around the five boroughs. Tonight, Madison had felt like dancing.

The couple made their way to the bar, where Steve ordered two Coronas. They sipped their beers in silence, gazing at the variety of New Yorkers who circled the room. The same-sex couples mixed and mingled with the straight ones, while the preppie college kids shared drinks with the Bohemian old-heads.

When a gorgeous blonde approached them and began chatting Madison up, Steve stared in wide-eyed wonder as the woman made a blatant pass at his companion as if he weren't standing there. Steve had never considered himself the jealous or insecure type, but he had to acknowledge that the woman was striking and, hey, this was the new millennium. It occurred to him that he didn't know enough about Madison to know specifically what she was in to and decided he wasn't about to take any chances. He placed a defensive arm around Madison's waist and pulled her to the dance floor. Madison's admirer followed them with burning eyes for a while before moving on in search of a new conquest.

"Well, Mr. Elliott, let's see what kind of moves you've got. Now you know this isn't ballroom dancing. I hope you can keep up," Madison teased.

"I've got moves, baby, believe that," he stated with the self-assuredness that she had grown used to hearing from him.

The beat pulsed loudly in their ears, sucking them into

it as their bodies moved against one another. They danced through song after song, laughing and teasing as they grew familiar with the movement of each other's bodies. Steve looked down at Madison, captivated by the sexiness of her frame as much as by the femininity she exuded without even trying. The skirt she wore exposed legs that held a promise that could not be denied. He ran his hands up and down her diminutive waist, settling on her hips, which were swaying against him at a melodic tempo.

Their bodies met, finding a comfortable space to claim as their own. The lights zipped across the dance floor, flashing on her golden skin, now covered with a thin layer of perspiration, and Steve realized that he had never met a woman whom he found more alluring. His arousal as they danced grew from deep inside and by the time it became a physical wanting, it was larger than the room itself. Their eyes locked and held as they both became aware of the desire that was building between them. Steve ran his hand across the soft locks that framed her face, delighting in the texture and feel of them against his skin. Steve's desire to kiss her, to taste her mouth and tongue, was stronger than any other urge he'd ever felt. Cupping her face in his hands and moving in slow motion, he bent his head toward hers and found a sweet mouth waiting in anticipation for him. His tongue tentatively pried its way in between her lips, making contact with her tongue in an almost timid fashion. She opened her mouth wider, allowing him deeper access, and he responded by giving her all of his tongue. Their kiss engaged every bit of their oral cavities, as they drew one another in to completely discover their essences.

Forgetting time and space, the gyrating bodies around

them became a distant memory, they moved to a place in their minds that was far removed from anything recognizable. Their ragged breathing was louder in their ears than the music, and everyone else in the room seemed to disappear at once, leaving them alone within their passion. The probing exploration of their tongues spurred them to greater desire until finally Steve pulled away, unable to take one more second of tortured provocation. He wanted to get her alone, and it was that single thought that drove him silently through the throngs of people and out onto the street.

Leaving the club arm in arm, they maintained the electrifying connection that had exploded between them. Madison settled against Steve's side as they drove back uptown to her place. With her eyes closed, she replayed the images of the two of them together, still warm from the heat their bodies had generated on the dance floor. When Steve found an empty parking spot right outside Madison's building, it was she who wordlessly took him by the hand and led him up the stairs to her third-story apartment.

They stood just inside the entryway of her apartment, staring at one another in the thick darkness. They both recognized the importance of their next steps and as they weighed the implications in their minds, they were overwhelmingly aware of the current that connected them. Somehow, Madison found the presence of mind to pause, a task that was equally difficult and unwanted.

"Are we moving too fast?" Madison asked at last, looking into Steve's eyes.

"Yes, we are," he answered truthfully, as he moved closer to her, still compelled to be near her.

Steve, like many young men of his age, had had his share of casual affairs. Yet he knew, without fully understanding why, that Madison could not be classified in that way. There would be no way that he could share her bed and just walk away, because she had already infected his heart in a way that no woman had ever managed to do. For her part, Madison was not a virgin and did not possess any virginlike ideals that made her desirous of resisting her sexuality or her body's longings. However, she was also aware that Steve had gotten under her skin, and sharing her body with him would not come without strings and entanglements. Neither could pretend that the feelings they were caught up in were not incredibly intense and moving.

"We probably should think this through," she whispered, her lips brushing across his as she spoke.

"Probably," he agreed, his hand kneading the small of her back softly. "Madison, I want you…badly," Steve laughed.

"Me, too."

"This is so difficult!" Steve exclaimed. "Look, I don't get what's going on here, but I just feel like it's too important to mess it up by rushing things."

"And sometimes sex does just that," Madison agreed.

As much as they wanted to take their desire to a higher level, the intimacy between them was compelling enough without an act of sexual intercourse. They paused to allow logic to take up a space in the midst of their excitement and found the consolation to be just as sweet as the first place prize when they spent the night fully clothed, snuggled against one another on Madison's brushed-cotton, oversized sofa. They talked until they feel asleep, and when they awoke in each other's arms, the satisfaction that washed over them made them both realize that they could not have felt more complete than they did by just being in one another's presence.

That languid bubble of tranquility was unexpectedly burst the following morning, however, when the *New York Post*'s gossip column featured a picture of them leaving the club the night before, arm in arm, with a caption beneath it that read, "Has Madison Daniels finally snagged herself a well-appointed Prince Charming?"

The columnist went on to report that this was the second known sighting of Madison and Stevenson Elliott, son of English billionaire Gregory Elliott.

"Do you believe this crap?" Madison spewed angrily.

"Perhaps you want to tell me over breakfast why the press is so fascinated with you?" Steve asked gently after he'd read the article that Madison had dropped on his lap.

Madison slid down onto the sofa beside him. "Look, me and the media have had a little love/hate thing going on for the past couple of years—they love to stay in my business, and I despise the wombs they came out of. Those people are animals and for some reason, they seem to find my little boring life of major interest, go figure."

"Somehow I doubt there is anything boring about your life," Steve said.

"Yeah, well, be that as it may, it just kills me that when a man dates and is linked to noteworthy women, he's this year's eligible bachelor. When it's the other way around, the woman's called every kind of gold-digging whore in the book."

"I agree. There's definitely a double standard, and I don't care what side of the globe you're on. But, in all fairness, the media only report on what people want to know, so don't blame them because we live in a society that is nosy and filthy-minded. And speaking of filthy…"

Steve tugged at the top of the tank top Madison wore. She smacked his hand.

"Seriously, Steve. I don't know if it's such a good idea that you and I be seen in public again. I mean, if this crap gets back to England, your parents might be a little, well, put off."

"Put off about what? That I've met a beautiful woman and am having the time of my life getting to know her?" Steve asked as he traced Madison's collarbone with two fingers.

"How about the fact that you're spending time with a woman who the press likes to spy on and paint to be some sort of strumpet who's out to trick him out of his family's fortune?"

"In that case, come here, my little strumpet," Steve said, pulling Madison across his body. "Let me teach you a lesson about stealing, you naughty girl."

Steve closed his mouth over hers, cutting off any further protests she could make.

## Chapter 7

"This is a nice hotel, but you've got a really crappy view," Madison said as she peered out of the fourteenth-floor window of Steve's hotel room.

He'd invited her to have dinner in with him that evening in acquiescence to her desire to keep their business out of the papers. A quiet evening indoors and out of the public eye was extremely appealing to both of them.

Steve moved to her side and looked through the glass himself. His room faced a parking garage and an office building. Looking to the left, he was afforded a partial view of the Times Square area, the lights from Broadway already brilliantly lighting up the street.

"Good thing it wasn't the view of New York City that I stayed in town for," he mused, having turned his attention away from the window and refocused it on the breathtaking woman standing beside him.

Madison smiled up at him, still amazed to find herself tingling under his gaze. It had been two weeks since they'd met and she was getting to believe that no matter how much time passed, she would still be as flattered by his considerate and charming nature as she was now.

"Are you ready for dinner?" he asked.

"Uh-uh," Madison answered as she moved closer to him.

She had an irresistible urge to kiss him and dinner would just have to wait until she satisfied that compulsion. She tilted her head, her lips angled a couple of inches away from his. When their mouths met, she felt her body tremble quietly. Her mouth opened to his probing tongue, and warmth spread through her entire body. Tentatively, yet expertly, he explored her mouth, breathing her in until she filled all of his senses. The thickness of his lips as she nibbled and tasted them caused her breath to catch in her throat while the heat of his tongue as it danced with hers sent an electric current straight down to the center of her taut abdomen.

Madison had kissed many men in her lifetime, but could honestly say that she had never been kissed so thoroughly and completely as Steve kissed her. She'd experienced passion and lust, she'd thrown herself with reckless abandoned into physical encounters and, while finding physical satisfaction, she realized now that the intimacy of a simple kiss with Steve far outweighed any of that. She lost herself inside his mouth, sank into his arms and discovered it was a restorative and peaceful place to be.

When their lips finally parted, Steve continued to hold her in his arms, her body resting against his as they stood in front of a window with a partial view of Manhattan. The serenity that settled over them made them both realize that what had begun as a chance meeting and an instant attraction had quickly morphed into something more profound than either had ever experienced before.

"I want to make love to you, Madison," Steve said, breaking the silence that had enveloped them.

"I hear a *but* in your voice," she responded.

Madison's heart raced because she'd already expected this moment, anticipated it, even. She felt the same way, a desire to share on a physical level what was developing on an emotional level. However, for the first time, she'd met someone and sexual curiosity was not the most pressing thing for her.

"But I'm not sure if we should. I mean, I want to. Don't get me wrong, I really, really want to," Steve laughed.

"Really?" Madison joked.

"Really, really," Steve reiterated. "I just…I've got to be honest with you."

"About what? Please don't tell me you've got a wife and three kids back in England, 'cause that's the last thing I need to hear in my life at this point," she said half-jokingly.

"Of course not. I'm single and unattached…no girlfriend, wife. Nothing like that. Actually, I haven't even been on a date in the past couple of months. It's just that, well, Madison, I've never felt like this before. I mean, these past two weeks have been incredible. Being here with you, it just totally caught me off guard, and I feel like I don't know whether I'm coming or going."

"I know what you mean."

"Do you?"

"Of course. Steve, you're definitely not out here on your own. I wasn't expecting this and after the last crazy couple of years I had, I certainly wasn't looking to hook up with anyone. But this is so different. With you I feel like I can just be myself and be however crazy, goofy or silly I feel like being. I don't have to be what my parents expect, I don't have to live up to what the media think about me and I don't have to give a damn about what my friends or anyone else asks of me. This has been so nice, but…" Madison's voice trailed off.

"But you think it has to end," Steve finished for her.

"Doesn't it? I mean, you have a life in England. I'm here trying to get my life together. You have obligations to keep. I mean, we just met. We're practically strangers."

Madison moved away from Steve, needing to distance herself from feelings that had come on too strong too soon. She stopped in front of the television, where some ridiculous commercial about a goat and a soft drink was playing.

"You don't feel like a stranger to me," Steve said as he watched her from his vantage point by the window.

The sincerity in his voice forced Madison to turn to face him. His face was an open book, free for her to read in his warm-brown eyes and sensual lips an emotion that was greater than lust and infatuation.

"You feel like home to me," he added softly.

Steve walked across the room to Madison, taking both of her hands in his. She allowed him to guide her to the top of the double bed, her body at his command as he lay down and pulled her with him. He leaned his back against the pillows, his arms around her, and she laid her head on his chest, listening to the sound of his breathing. Wrapped in a cocoon isolated from the outside world, they felt free to be real with each other.

"I don't know how to explain what I am feeling right now and I don't even really understand it, but it's like I was looking for something or needing something and all of a sudden I don't feel that need anymore," Steve said softly.

"It's scary how connected I feel to you already, Steve," Madison admitted. "I think I've been looking for something, too, without even knowing it."

They fell silent, alone with their thoughts yet sharing an emotion that was bigger than both of them. A long while later Steve spoke, his meditation having taken him to a place deep inside in his soul.

"When I was a little boy, maybe four or five, I remember sitting on my grandmother's rocker on the veranda of her house. Grandma's house was old like most of the houses in the countryside of Jamaica where we lived. You know, outhouses and open-air cooking."

"Hmm," Madison said.

"Grandma was standing over the cooking fire making cornmeal porridge in a big metal pot that was situated on a metal grate and held up on a pile of big rocks. She had on a floral house dress and these tattered brown sandals. I had been helping Grandpa tie the livestock out in the hills like we did every morning and was sitting down to catch my breath. I started telling her how Uncle Nevel had promised to take me fishing at Alligator Pond early the next morning. I bragged and bragged about how I was going to catch the biggest fish of all, bigger even than the one Uncle Nevel had caught the week before, and I was going to bring it back to her to cook it up for dinner."

Steve paused, and stared out into space for a moment. Madison waited, stroking the back of his hand gently.

"When Grandma turned around, her face was wet. She was smiling at me, but tears were streaming down her face. I went over to her. I was only four but my head already reached Grandma's chin. I remember asking her if she wanted to go fishing with us…if that's why she was crying. That question made her laugh out loud. She had a soft tinkling laugh. She laughed and hugged me, rocking me against her body. I was so confused. But then she told me that no matter what happened, no matter how far away I went or how big I got, I would always be her *best lickle pickney*…her favorite little child."

Madison looked up at Steve, saw the tear that had formed in the corner of his left eye. His face was pained and she wanted to ask why, but she also wanted to give him the space and time to tell his story the way he needed to.

"She sat down in the rocker and held me on her lap, telling me all the while that I was getting too big to sit all over her like that."

Steve fingered one of the twists of hair that covered Madison's head. "Grandma had worn dreadlocks, too, but hers were long and thick from years of growing. I started playing with her hair like I always did and she just held me, bouncing me up and down on her knee and staring down at me like she was trying to capture me in her mind.

"Two days later, my dad came back from a trip to England and a few days after that my parents and I left Jamaica. I didn't know it at the time, but that would be the last time I saw my grandmother. We left our warm, sunny island where I spent long days chasing butterflies and swimming in the creek and we moved to England. Everybody I'd spent my childhood with—my grandmother, my grandfather, uncles, aunts and a dozen cousins—were left behind. I spoke to Grandma by phone a couple of times…on her birthday and Christmas, you know? I always asked her when she was coming to visit and she kept saying that she didn't like to fly."

"Why didn't you guys ever go back to Jamaica?" Madison asked.

"I don't know," Steve said, chewing on the question as if its answer was the secret to the universe. "My parents always made up excuses when I asked. They were too busy with the business. It wasn't the right time. And no one could come to visit us because we didn't have space for them at first. Eventually, I guess when they thought I was old enough, they told me that our relatives were better off in Jamaica. They said that they could never fit in with our new, prosperous lives in England. I didn't understand this philosophy of theirs until much later on in life. It seemed the wealthier we became, the less we associated with anyone who was Jamaican. My parents made sure I lost my accent quickly, and essentially, we cut all ties with that part of our heritage. We became English citizens and that was that."

"That's terrible," Madison said, thinking of her own parents and their separatist ways.

"For a long time, I've wondered why I allowed them to do that to me. Don't get me wrong, I'm not one of those people who you see on those daytime talk shows talking about their horrible upbringings and neglectful parents. I mean, I had a great childhood. I had privileges that most kids only dream about. I went to good schools and traveled to exotic places. But part of me always felt guilty when I thought about the family we'd left back in Jamaica. Life can be hard in the islands."

"Steve, you were a child. How could you possibly have done anything to change the situation?"

"Not then, but as I got older…in my teen years. I should have done something. When Grandma died, we didn't even go to the funeral."

The broken expression on Steve's face caused Madison to want to capture him completely in her arms and kiss his wounds away.

"How long ago did she pass away?" she asked softly.

"I was sixteen. I remember my parents were planning a holiday, and I suggested that we go to Jamaica. They scoffed at that idea. I'd started asking questions about Jamaica and the family back there and that's when my father told me that there wasn't much family left. He said it almost matter-of-factly. Maybe five or six months later, we received a phone call…I think it was from one of my father's brothers. Grandma had passed in her sleep at the age of seventy-two. I thought we would go to the funeral, but we didn't. My mother explained that my father was too busy to leave work at that time, which of course didn't make much sense to me, but by then, I pretty much understood that they had no intentions of ever setting foot there again. So when my grandfather followed her a year later, I wasn't surprised that we didn't go to his funeral, either."

"Are you still afraid of what your parents will say if you make contact with your family now?"

Steve looked down at Madison.

"You think I'm a coward, don't you?" he asked, a nervous chuckle pushing through his lips.

"No, I don't think that at all," Madison said, stroking the side of his face thoughtfully. "I think you are a loyal and considerate man, who worries too much about doing the right thing and doing what his parents want him to do. I know this is not the same thing, but one truth I have learned recently is that while everything we do will have consequences, we're the only ones we have to seek approval from."

"Perhaps you're right," Steve said.

He buried his chin in the top of Madison's head and closed his eyes.

"Sometimes it's hard to follow your own voice," he said, his voice now thick with drowsiness.

In the past few days his dreams and conscious thoughts had been filled with a mixture of Madison and images of Jamaica and his grandmother. It was as if his meeting Madison had caused remembrances that he had buried long ago to resurface. Strange as it seemed, he pondered if Madison had come in to his life at this time for the sole purpose of helping him to remember.

"She would have liked you," he said.

"Maybe one day I can get to see where you lived with her," Madison said.

"Maybe," Steve echoed, his eyes closed and his arms wrapped tightly around Madison, as if he never intended to let her go.

It was just that rapidly and with ease that his soul connected with hers and the comfort that he felt as he lay tangled in her embrace was strangely familiar to him. They'd come from different soil and circumstances, but shared upbringings that were symmetrical in ways that made them understand one another. Minutes seemed like days, days like months, until the length of time that had passed since the moment of their meeting could not be comprehended as being short or limited. All either one of them knew was that they would be forever changed by their meeting.

# Chapter 8

"This is not a love thing," Madison said as she wound the leash of Brandy, a ninety-five-pound golden retriever, tightly around her hand.

Her shoes slapped against the pavement as Chip, the fifty-pound sleek black Doberman, pulled her toward a cluster of trees that had attracted his attention. The two dogs and a lady made quite a trio. This was one of the various odd jobs that Madison worked in order to supplement the monthly allowance her father provided. She enjoyed walking dogs the most because it was a job that obligated her to remain out of doors for stretches at a time instead of being cooped up in an office or building. The dogs both lived in buildings in her neighborhood and she'd been their official exercise and relief chief for the past three months. While both dogs busied themselves sniffing at the shrubbery that lined the small park, Madison adjusted the Bluetooth earpiece against the side of her head.

"Sounds like it to me," her sister Kennedy said into her ear.

Madison and Kennedy had been close growing up, but had gone through an estrangement over the past few years that Madison knew had more to do with her own reckless behavior than with anything Kennedy had or had not done. She celebrated the fact that in recent months they had begun talking more regularly and sharing more of their lives with each other just like back in the old days. Having her sister in her life as a confidante was one of the highlights of her newly structured existence, because as headstrong as Madison had always been, she still appreciated the value of having her big sister's wisdom to call on from time to time.

"Just because you're all lovey-dovey with that husband of yours doesn't mean that you should try to paint the rest of the world with that same brush," Madison replied.

"Methinks the lady doth protest too much," Kennedy said, donning a poor imitation of a British accent.

"Very funny, Kennedy. Where are you anyway?"

"Right now I am at the folks' house. I just came back from Dad's office. We had lunch and then I looked over some papers for him. He's thinking about buying in to this retirement community idea that one of his club members is developing."

"Oh, and where's Malik?"

"Malik is at home in D.C. He's driving down to meet me on Friday. We're going to spend the weekend here. You know Saturday is Aunt Marva's fiftieth birthday party. I heard you're not planning to come."

"No, I don't feel like traveling all the way down there. Besides, I've got a ton of things to do. Make sure you give her my regards."

"Uh-huh…you've got a ton of things to do all right. I bet you they all revolve around that man," Kennedy teased.

"Not even," Madison said, not sounding very convincing to even her own ears.

"Oh, Maddie, what's the big deal? What would be so wrong with admitting that you've fallen in love with this guy? Mom told me that he's gorgeous and very nice."

"Your mother has a big mouth. She's only seen him one time…she barely exchanged two words with him. How would she know? Anyway, that's not even the point."

"What is the point then?"

"I'll tell you what the point is. Are you listening? Because I'm going to tell you what the point is. The point is that…well, the point is that—"

"You have no point. You met a guy who's different from every guy you've ever met. You're attracted to him on a level that you've never really reached before with anyone else, not counting Chucky Denton in the fifth grade, and you, my dear, are at a loss as to what to do about it. Does that about sum up your dilemma?"

"I cannot believe you brought up Chucky Denton, of all people. I thought we agreed that neither one of us would ever mention that fat, freckle-faced jerk or the fact that he stood me up for the spring dance so he could take that buck-toothed, big, barrel-behind girl, Tracee Alston, simply because everybody knew she would let you get a whole lot more than a kiss during a game of R.C.K.," Madison shot back.

"Oops, my bad, girl. I didn't realize that you were still so upset over Chu—I mean, that boy. But forget about that. Let's focus and get back to the right here and right now. Steve. Do you want to tell me what the problem really is, Maddie?"

Madison slid down to the grass next to Brandy and Chip. It was the time of morning when the sun was still friendly. She could feel the cool grass beneath her thighs, which were exposed thanks to the navy blue terry cloth shorts she wore. Today was promising to be a hot day and she hoped to have finished all of her errands and be back indoors, enjoying the central air conditioning of her apartment by the time the sun reached its full strength.

Chip immediately lay down beside her, rolled onto his back to expose his belly in the hopes that he could get a free rub. Madison obliged absently while Brandy continued sniffing at the trees and grass, paying no attention whatsoever to either Madison or her fellow four-legged friend.

"I really like him, Kennedy. A lot," Madison admitted.

It was the first time she'd allowed herself to say those words aloud, acknowledging how deeply she had grown to feel about Steve.

"That's great, Madison. I don't see why that's such a big problem."

"Well for starters, I just met him like not even three weeks ago. I mean, you know I have a bad habit of jumping in to things impulsively. How do I know that I'm not doing the same thing that I said I wasn't going to do anymore all over again?"

"Have you slept with him yet?" Kennedy asked.

"No. We've talked about it, but we both thought it would be better if we didn't."

"Hmph, sounds to me like you've found yourself a really great guy… One who thinks with the head upstairs instead of the one downstairs. That's definitely two points for the brother and for you too, little sis. Isn't that a sign that you're not being impulsive?"

"I guess. It's just crazy for me to be having these feelings so fast, isn't it?"

"Maybe at one time I would have agreed with that, but after what I went through last year, nothing in this world would surprise me. After my accident, the last thing I thought would happen would be that I would meet someone and fall in love, but it happened. Malik and I could be voted most unlikely couple for as different as we are, but you know what? At the end of the day, you've got to be able to sit down and realize that none of that matters when it's true love. Madison, you can't predict when, how or with whom it's going to happen. It doesn't work that way."

"But he's got responsibilities back home. He can't stay here forever."

"So what, Maddie? You've got a passport and it's not like you have a steady job that you are committed to."

"Is that a dig, Kennedy?" Madison asked indignantly.

While she couldn't deny that she was not known for being a career woman like Kennedy, she really didn't appreciate any sort of snide commentary about that fact.

"Not at all. I'm just saying that it can work if you want it to. You'll visit. He'll visit. Instead of making up excuses, you should just be enjoying this and seeing how it goes. For goodness' sake, stop putting up roadblocks in your own way."

Madison considered her sister's words for a moment, weighing the pros and cons of a long-distance relationship with Steve. She decided that the pros far outweighed the cons, starting with the fact that despite what she'd told Kennedy, the man already had her heart in the palm of his hands. Walking away now would have been difficult, and it was not something that she had any inclination to do.

"You're right, Kennedy. I'm just going to chill out and see what happens."

"There's my girl. So when am I going to get to meet this millionaire of yours?"

"Correction, he's a billionaire," Madison laughed. "Nah, I'm just joking. Steve will be the first one to tell you that it's his father who is rich, not him. Anyway, he doesn't need his daddy's money because he's smart and motivated and he'd be successful on his own."

"Aww, look at you. Aren't you just the little cheerleader."

"Shut up, Kennedy."

Madison chatted with Kennedy for a while longer, soaking up the sisterly advice that she gave. She realized that it wouldn't hurt to just keep kicking it with Steve, taking things at a leisurely pace and seeing what happened. After all, it wasn't every day that she met a single, heterosexual and upwardly mobile black man who was interested in getting to know her from the neck up only.

# Chapter 9

"Mother, it's not like that," Steve said.

He turned away from Madison, moving across the room. It was a futile effort, however, because in the tiny room there was nowhere he could go to maintain a private conversation. Madison moved closer to the window, staring outside without really seeing. She knew exactly what his mother was saying to him without having to hear the woman's voice.

"No, Mother. No. You are exaggerating as usual and—"

Steve breathed heavily into the phone.

"You can't believe everything you read, Mother."

The volume of Steve's voice rose ever so slightly. He then fell silent for a few moments.

"Hello, sir…yes, sir…I know, I know."

Steve glanced at Madison, who kept her back turned to him.

She didn't need to see him to know that he was trying hard to appear to be having a casual conversation, when all the while the rhythm of his words and his body language belied that effort.

"I know she's upset, but she really has no reason to be. I…soon, sir."

Steve was silent for a full minute as his father railed on and on.

"No. All right. Good night."

Steve hung up the telephone heavily. He sat down on the edge of the bed, still holding the phone in his hands. The room was thick with a silence that choked them both. It was Madison who finally broke the hush.

"Parents not too happy about what the rags are reporting, huh?" she asked without turning around.

Steve studied her back, the rigidity of her posture apparent even from across the room. He rested the phone on the floor and rose, his steps deliberate as he went to her. He stopped directly behind her, close enough to touch her but not doing so.

"They'll get over it," he said softly.

Madison turned to face him, looking into brown eyes that still made her knees feel weak.

"You don't even believe that yourself," she answered.

"Madison—"

"Stop, Steve, just stop."

"Okay, you're right. They've seen the headlines and the photos and they are very upset. You've got to understand something. My parents are very private people. They don't like to see their family name being dragged through the tabloids. Can you blame them for that?"

"No, I can't blame them at all. However, I've come to understand that when you let the trash that gets printed about you get under your skin, you're allowing those irresponsible and inconsiderate jackasses to win. If you just ignore it and don't give any fuel to their fire, it will go away."

"Unfortunately, my parents haven't had much experience with this sort of thing. They want me to come home right away."

Madison studied Steve's face for a moment. She shook her head in dismay, throwing up both of her hands.

"I'm leaving," she said, brushing past him hastily.

"What? Where are you going?" Steve asked.

"Home, and I suggest you do the same. It's been real," she said as she snatched her purse from the desk and stormed toward the door.

She was determined to make it out of that room and out of his sight before he could see her and read the devastation written all over her face.

"Hold on," Steve shouted as he dashed after her. He stopped her at the door as she fumbled to turn the doorknob. "Would you stop this, Madison? Just stop for one minute," he said.

"What is it, Steve? There's really nothing left to say. Your parents don't want you to have anything to do with me and frankly, it's probably for the best."

"What the hell is that supposed to mean—*for the best?*"

"Look, we've had fun, haven't we? We both knew from the start that this wasn't going to be anything more than that. I guess it was our mistake that we didn't screw, but better luck next time, huh?"

Madison hurled her words at him, wanting to repel him

and make him back away from her. She'd have done anything to get him to step aside and allow her to leave while she still could. Instead, he grabbed her by the shoulders, pulling her sharply to him.

"First of all, don't you dare talk to me in that way. Don't you try to push me away like I'm just some guy you met and don't stand here and try to pretend that this was just some sort of fling…some—some sort of casual affair and that's it. It's more than that to me, much more than that, and I know it means more to you, too."

"See, that's just it, Steve, you think you know me, but you don't. You don't know the things I've done…the men, the drugs or the incessant partying. You think the papers write about me just for the fun of it? Huh? Is that what you think?" Madison shouted back, hurling her words in his face forcefully.

"I don't give a bloody hell what the papers have to say about you. I couldn't care less if you were a holy virgin or the whore of Babylon. What you did before we met is none of my damned business. It's you, Madison…it's you and me…right now is all I care about. My God," Steve exclaimed, backing away from Madison and banging his back against the door. "I ought to have my head examined. Can't you see what you've done to me?"

"You don't know me, Steve," she whispered, unable to find the strength and conviction she'd had a few moments before.

"Then tell me. Tell me who you are. Let me get to know all of you, Madison."

Madison could no longer fight back the tears that welled up in her eyes. The anguish on Steve's face was undeniable and it matched the turmoil that she felt inside her own heart.

"Steve, I'm just a mixed-up girl trying to find her way. You and I are so different. You've known who you were and what you were supposed to do since you were a kid. You've learned your family business and will be a powerful executive soon, overseeing a billion-dollar corporation. You were a good student and are a great businessman. Me? Me, I'm just trying to step out from beneath my parent's thumb and be my own person, but I have a long way to go. I'm trying to become a woman…my own woman, and before I can figure out what I have to offer you or anybody else, I've got to determine what I have to offer myself."

"Madison, don't you see that that is precisely why I'm so attracted to you? You are not afraid to step out and claim what you want from this world. You're not ashamed of who you are or who you've been during this learning process. You are a woman who is strong, determined and courageous. A woman who has the power to hold her man up when he needs it and that's the kind of woman I need because, despite what you may think, Madison, I'm not so strong. Every day I have questions about myself and my purpose. When I'm with you, I'm free to talk or be silent, to laugh or to sulk. I have not felt this kind of freedom in all my life, and I'm not about to let it go. Madison, I'm in love with you," he said, his eyes intent.

He moved closer to her, reaching out to delicately shift one of the silky locks of hair that had fallen onto her forehead.

"Tell me that you don't feel the same way as I do, and I'll step aside and let you leave this room right now," he said cautiously.

Madison bit her bottom lip, trying to keep her eyes from making contact with his. But the pull was too strong and she found herself staring into his liquid pools.

"I can't," she whispered in spite of the knowledge that they should not be together.

They folded into one another's arms, their hearts racing as they realized that they had just taken a step from which there was no turning back. When Steve's phone rang again, no doubt a summons from his parents, they ignored it.

# Chapter 10

"I'm going to call you as soon as I land tomorrow night," Steve said.

"That's fine," Madison answered.

They were strolling up Seventy-fourth Street, hand in hand, after having spent the past couple of hours at the movies. The melancholy mood that had settled over him since his parents' angered phone calls and their insistence that he return to England immediately had become too much to bear and they'd decided to go out to see a new comedy starring Vince Vaughn and Owen Wilson, two of Steve's favorites. They'd laughed considerably during the movie and their spirits had been lifted. The short walk back to Madison's apartment was filled with casual chatter, each of them wanting desperately to avoid the subject of Steve's impending departure.

## Chapter 2

The abrupt flash of a photographer's camera snatched Madison and Steve from their private thoughts, bringing them back to the crowded roomful of people, music and laughter. Before either could react, they found themselves flanked on either side by reporters and cameras.

"Madison Daniels, rumor has it that now that Felicia Worthington has withdrawn the divorce papers, you and Edward Worthington have taken it as a license to resume your relationship. Care to comment?"

Madison's eyes were trained on the smiling, fire-engine-red lipsticked mouth of the reporter who was thrusting a black microphone into her face, almost touching her nose with it.

"Wha-what?" she stuttered, unable to compose herself.

rhythm of the other. It was as if a spell had been cast over them, and quite like Cinderella and the prince at the royal ball, they were frozen in an enchanted spell. Those precious magic minutes were the stuff dreams were made of, and although neither one of them had been looking, the discovery was welcome just the same.

At Madison's doorstep, she leaned in to him, burying her face in his chest.

"I want you to come up," she said without looking at him.

"If I come up, I'm not leaving until morning," he declared, his words a firm statement backed with desire.

They made their way upstairs in silence, both of them understanding the implied terms of their decision. Inside, Madison led Steve to her bedroom. Once there, instead of turning on the lights, she lit the variety of candles that adorned the room.

Steve's breath came in short bursts against her neck as she leaned her back against his trembling chest. His arms were locked around her body, trapping her in his embrace. She ran her hands up and down his forearms, the soft hair that covered them tickling her palms. Steve moved his nose across the top of her hair, inhaling deeply the scent of aloe vera and citrus that escaped from the short locks that made her look so much like the women of his youth, despite her fair complexion. He pulled her tight-fitting black T-shirt, embossed with the words *Run, Catch and Kiss Me,* over her head. The softness of her skin against his was as incredible as he'd imagined it would be. He cupped her breasts, filling up his hands with them and squeezing as they strained against her bra, as if wanting to jump out into the open. Madison arched her back and bent her head backward so that she could reach his warm, waiting lips. His deep kisses grew deeper and more intense as he turned her around to face him. She backed slightly away, slowly undoing each button of his shirt. He dropped his hands to his sides, allowing her to undress him, peeling back his layers as one would the skin of an orange. First she slid the shirt away from his shoulders, then it was his pants that joined the shirt on the floor. As he stood there in black briefs, his desire for her was discernible even in the dim candlelit room. He tugged at his underpants, stepping out of them to expose an instrument that was aimed and ready to give pleasure.

"I want to know if you taste as sweet as you look," he said huskily.

He pushed Madison backward until she dropped onto the king-sized bed, cool Egyptian cotton sheets welcoming her sizzling flesh. Steve spread his length beside her, planting warm kisses on her. He visited every square inch of her face, ears and neck, leaving his mark everywhere his hot lips landed. He traveled downward, smoothly freeing her aching breasts from their confinement. Her breath caught at the sight of her swollen nipples, like two ripe berries just waiting to be plucked. And he did, over and over again, using his mouth to caress the circumference of her nipples until they were engorged and raw with craving. He blazed a trail down her flat stomach, sucking at her belly button.

"You've got an outie," he stated as he tongued the thin line of hair that led to the white satin boy shorts she wore.

"Mmm-hmm," she murmured in anticipation.

Steve shifted his body, placing himself directly between her legs. He grasped the silky fabric of her panties, snatching them down and pulling them off her eagerly with one hand. An image of how she'd looked dancing a few nights before at the club so seductively against him flashed before his eyes. He'd wanted her so much then and it was as if that desire had stayed with him, growing and filling him up until he felt that he would drown in it. He did not want to wonder any longer what her thighs would feel like around his face. He grabbed her hips to still her squirming bottom. The soft triangular tuft of hair that surrounded her mound tickled his nose as he sniffed, inhaling the sexy scent of her womanhood. He kissed her bud and she gasped audibly, her sounds coming from the depths of her. He kissed it again, more firmly this time, and she trembled. She tried to arch her hips to meet his face, but he held fast, controlling the pace of his exploration.

"Steve," she whispered.

"Shhh," he commanded.

He introduced his tongue to her warm center, slowly and deliberately. As her body began to shake and convulse, he dined on her more rapidly, deriving as much pleasure from her moans of satisfaction as she was getting from him. His tongue went deep, diving in like an expert underwater explorer. Inside her candy walls he found the answer to his question—she was twice as sweet as he had dreamed she would be.

He lapped and sucked without stopping, minute after pleasured agony-filled minute. The first waves of her climax shook them both. He held on tightly as her legs squeezed together around his face. When after several minutes her body quieted, he moved back to the top of the bed, stopping to visit her perky breasts again, their sienna peaks still standing at full attention. He thought at that moment he could spend the rest of his life dining on her breasts, each a mound of fleshy perfection. His throbbing manhood reminded him, however, that there were other parts of her that he wanted to visit.

"Protection?" he asked.

Madison stirred from the stupor his loving had placed her in. Every inch of her body tingled with satisfaction and with undulating longing. Her skin felt electrified, as if the tiny hairs that ran all along the surface had been plugged into a two-hundred-volt socket. She reached up to the tiny red velvet keepsake box that rested on the light bridge above her bed. From within she retrieved a gold package, which she handed to Steve.

"I don't know what the shelf life on those things is. I hope it hasn't expired... It's been a while," she explained.

Steve removed the latex glove, examined it briefly and slid it over his throbbing shaft. He rolled over onto his back, pulling Madison's tight body on top of him. He kissed her softly, ending with a firm suck on her delicious bottom lip.

"I want this to feel like your first time," he said at length.

Madison straddled him, sliding her body down onto his slowly. She felt her walls expand and contract around him, causing a shiver to run up and down her spine so sharply that she arched her back in response. Steve gasped, marveling at the tightness of her sugar nest as it closed around his thickness. When she began to move her body, he almost exploded immediately. He forced himself to count backward from ten in order to slow the rush that surged through him.

"What's the matter, baby?" Madison asked.

"Nothing. Nothing at all. You're perfect," he answered, reaching up to touch her face.

Their lovemaking was slow and intense, their bodies growing ever more familiar with each other. They found a rhythm that allowed them to drive each other to greater heights of pleasure than either had ever known. Sweat dripped from Madison's body onto Steve's, and when he pulled her down on top of him, wanting to feel her breasts pressing against his chest, the moisture of their bodies mingled with the heady scent of their sex. They rolled so that Madison's back now rested against the mattress. The pace of their lovemaking picked up as their desire for completion became more fervent. Finally, Steve let himself go, no longer holding back the fire that had been flaming inside him. He stiffened and erupted inside Madison. At his moment of release she, too, found herself trembling with liberation. It was a long time before they were able to come back to themselves and descend from the elevated place to which they'd soared.

Twelve hours later, Steve stared out of the miniature window in the first-class cabin of the British Airways jet as his plane taxied away from the gate to take its place on the runway. All he could see before him were visions of Madison as he'd left her that morning, tangled in sheets and still spent from their night of lovemaking. He'd had to fight with every fiber of his being to pull himself from her bed, and as he ascended through the sky now, he felt as though he'd left his soul on that mattress with her. Less than three hours after he'd left her, he was filled with a longing so profound that he contemplated leaping from the airplane while it was in midflight just to get back to her. He was certain that even without a parachute, his swollen heart would be enough to guide him safely back to the ground.

# Chapter 11

After an extended journey with a plane change in London, Steve landed at Liverpool's John Lennon Airport, which had been renamed in honor of the late pop icon of former Beatle fame in 2001. From the moment he arrived, his almost eight-hour flight having been an exhausting experience of restlessness and anxiety, his mind had been jumbled with conflicting thoughts. He'd been unable to get a direct flight back into Manchester, which would have been closer to his flat in that town, stretching his travel time out even more. It did not help matters that upon landing, he was filled with another feeling that was less welcome. He dreaded the confrontation he felt coming on with his parents. Yet he was confident that if they only took the time to hear him out, they would understand that he trusted his own judgment and, as such, so should they. Madison was not anything like what the gossip columnists had made her out to be. He was determined to make his parents see her in the way that he saw her.

His father's driver, Hayden, was waiting at the baggage claim area for him when he landed. Much to his annoyance, the airport was crowded and chaotic as usual. After his active night and long trip, Steve could think of nothing better to do than go back to his place, take a hot shower and sink into his bed. However, Hayden emphatically stated that he was under direction to bring Steve back to his parents' home promptly. It seemed that that hot shower would have to wait.

The Elliotts lived in Mossley Hill, one of Liverpool's most affluent suburbs located in Merseyside. Their estate was breathtaking, having been restored tremendously in the past five years as Steve's father gave in to each and every one of his mother's whims. Seated in the backseat of his father's CLK63 AMG Black Edition, Steve closed his eyes and thought of Madison. He attempted to settle his nerves by revisiting his time in her arms. The smile on her face and the flash of her eyes soothed him, but nothing could calm the storm of anxiety that brewed in the center of his gut.

"Son, I can't tell you how disturbing all of this has been to your mother and me," Gregory Elliott snapped the moment Steve had entered his study, shutting the door behind him.

"Hey, Dad. It's great to see you, too," Steve answered, annoyed that his father hadn't had the decency to at least offer him a drink first before lighting into him. "Has Mom gone to bed already?"

Steve walked over to the rolling bar in the corner of the room and poured himself a shot of Hennessy. He shot his father a look as he sauntered to the two-seater to the right of the massive mahogany desk where his father sat.

"Yes, she's been suffering from a migraine all day," Gregory Elliott said.

Janice Elliott had first begun experiencing migraines upon their arrival in England. The doctor who first examined her there had told her that her debilitating head-aches were probably the result of the stress of relocating. Of course, Gregory had dismissed the notion as rubbish, considering the fact that Janice had worked hard all of her life and, having grown up just as poor and disadvantaged as he, was no stranger to stress. However, as the years passed and Janice's migraines persisted, he softened. In an uncharacteristic show of consideration, he made a con-certed effort to keep her away from hassles and pressures, attempting to deal with many issues on his own. This time was no exception.

"Back in Jamaica I spent ten years working for a bauxite company, digging in the red dirt for ten hours every day. Every time I picked up a handful of that dirt, I saw more than what other people saw in it. I saw my future. I saw the richness and the potential for my life—one that would be bigger than drinking, sleeping around and dying poor by the age of fifty-five. I landed a job at Reynolds Metal, at that time one of the biggest producers of raw materials.

"When I moved your mother and you to England, I had an opportunity to leave all of that poverty and ignorance behind. I worked hard to become an executive and to contribute to the revolutionization of the industry. I spent

five years at Reynolds, learning and saving every penny
we could spare. When I launched the Elliott Corporation,
it was the equivalent of all of my dreams coming true. It
was as if all of the hard work had finally paid off.
Suddenly, I was able to give you and your mother everything I'd never had growing up. Don't you think for one
minute that you haven't had a better life because of my
sacrifices."

"I know that, Dad, and I appreciate all that you and
Mother have provided for me. But, Dad, I'm a grown man
now, and I need you to give me some space."

"Space? What do you need space for? To run around
with...with a Jezebel—"

"Watch it, Dad. Please don't disrespect her."

"Steve, you don't even know this woman and you're
talking about disrespecting her. You spent three weeks,
rolling around in the hay, no doubt, with this woman and
suddenly you think you should defend her honor, even if it
means disrespecting your own father. You need to take a
look at yourself, young man, and get a hold of your emotions.
Don't mistake a good lay for anything more than it is."

Steve gripped the lead crystal shot glass in his hand,
aching to raise his arm and send it across the room. He
fought the urge, grasping with great difficulty the knowledge that no matter how crass and insulting his father could
be, he was still his father.

"Look, son, I don't mean to be crude, but I want you to
take a moment to think...really think about the rest of your
life. You are a young man who has an auspicious future
ahead of you. How many men your age can boast a net
worth as considerable as yours? You are a catch that many

young woman will dip their rods in the water for in the hopes of snagging you. You have to be careful."

"Dad, you've been telling me this all of my life. Don't you think I know all of that stuff? But here's something that you don't know—Madison is nothing like what the papers say about her and, besides, she doesn't need my money. Her father is a renowned cosmetic surgeon and Madison, well, she's going to be great at whatever she decides to do for a career. She's smart and courageous—"

"Steve, I don't want to argue this with you anymore. You have responsibilities here. We're taking on a great challenge in assuming the operations of Wesco and it's going to require around-the-clock preparations and negotiations. The last thing you need to trouble yourself with is trying to carry on some casual relationship with a woman who lives on the other side of the globe. Now, there will be no more of this business. I don't want your mother upset any more than she already is. Is that understood?"

Steve did not respond. His anger would not let him say anything more. He sat in his father's study long after the elder Elliott had retired for the night. In the dim lamplight, the room was an exact representation of the man—dark colors, expensive articles and clutter-free. Every item in the room had been hand-selected and fitted with precision in its place. The framed photographs on the walls were black-and-whites of historic landmarks in Europe and the United States, including the Eiffel Tower and the Statue of Liberty. The carpet was a rich blend of wine and golden hues, and the walls had been covered with a soft, fabric like wallpaper of muted sand color. On the mahogany desk rested a mother-of-pearl gemstone globe with table clock and thermometer, which Steve had always been fascinated by. The globe, which measured six inches in diameter, had been handcrafted with a variety of natural semiprecious stones such as tiger eye, abalone shell, onyx and, Steve's personal favorite, jade. On it many of the countries were labeled, as well as some capitals and other large cities. Beneath the globe sat a four-sided mechanism housing three different clocks designed to keep track of time in different parts of the world. The clocks contained crystals to mark the hours and a thermometer that measured the temperature in Fahrenheit and Centigrade. The rotating globe and clock were encircled by four brass pillars, all of which were mounted on a circular, golden-colored base that rotated. This clock was a small example of the luxuries the Elliotts surrounded themselves with as a token of the success they'd worked so hard to amass.

Also on the desk were a twenty-four-karat gold fountain pen, a leather-bound calendar and a shiny black telephone with headset. The tall-backed leather desk chair was pulled back from the desk a bit, to allow his father to slide his frame into the seat with ease. At this point in his career, Gregory Elliott was comfortable splitting his time between his well-equipped study, his office at corporate headquarters and at the two-hundred-acre plant where his company manufactured its products.

The burgundy leather sofa on which Steve now rested with his head thrown back squeaked under his shifted weight. He remembered the days as a young boy when he'd played quietly with his action figures on that very sofa while his father worked. Back then, he'd never grown tired of being around his father, who he'd thought was the wisest, most hardworking man in the world. He'd been proud to visit his father's job with him, watching as people jumped to his every command while he reigned as lord supreme over the plant and office. A lot had changed since then, and while Steve still held the utmost respect and admiration for all that his father had accomplished, having grown from a poor island boy into the head of his own billion-dollar corporation, there were many things about his father as a man that he disliked. Gregory Elliott could be downright cruel when he wanted to be, and because of the position he held, no one ever dared to challenge him or call him on his behavior.

Steve sighed as memories resurfaced of how his mother had often been the brunt of his father's cruel tongue and less than admirable actions. Steve never understood why she not only tolerated his father's behavior, but also often defended him. She was a dutiful wife and mother who acquiesced to her husband's every wish and command. To Steve, it appeared that his father did not value his mother's opinions or the things that she did to make his life comfortable as much as he professed to on the surface. Steve knew that he could never be content with a woman who could not put him in his place when he was out of line, but instead, remained the background to his foreground.

As Steve had grown in to manhood, and been groomed from birth to take over his father's empire, his heart began to move in a different direction. He doubted seriously if he could ever be the man his father was in business; more importantly, he questioned whether he truly wanted to or not. Meeting Madison only added to his dilemma as he realized that loving her might cost him much more than he was prepared to pay.

By the time he stumbled into his apartment, his head ached and his throat was raw from having held back all of the things that his heart had wanted to say to his father. He threw himself onto the sofa, unable to make it past his living room, and tossed and turned all night long. His guilt for not defending Madison more ferociously prevented him from getting a good night's rest.

Steve eventually came to the conclusion—after long, hard consideration—that the best course of action with his parents would be to say nothing for the time being. He would allow the dust to settle and let the tabloids find other more interesting subjects to devour before he expressed his feelings and his intentions toward Madison. He rationalized that that would give him time to figure out for himself exactly what those intentions were.

# Chapter 12

"Good morning, sleepyhead," Steve said.

"Steve? Oh, my goodness. What time is it?" Madison squealed into the phone.

She sat up in bed, clutching tangled sheets to her body. She'd tossed and turned all night, waiting for the telephone to ring and bring the sound of Steve's voice to her. She glanced over at the clock, noting that the time was a quarter past seven.

"It's just after twelve noon here, and I'm missing you like crazy already," Steve declared.

His night had been restless, his only comfort coming from thoughts of Madison. He longed to be back in her bed, cocooned by her warmth and her fragrant body. He'd give anything to turn back the hands of time, to rewind the clock so that he could be tangled in her arms and legs once again. The thought of her soft body pressed up against his was strong enough to bring him to erection, and sleeping had been quite difficult in that state.

"I miss you, too. How was your flight?"

"Uneventful."

"And your parents? I'll bet they were happy to see you."

"Well, the jury is still out on that. Actually, I haven't seen my mother yet. My father, well, I'll put it this way— he had a whole lot to say."

"I'll bet."

"I'm sorry I didn't call you when I got in. My father sent a car for me to come out to the house because he wanted to talk."

"I'll bet he gave you an earful," Madison said.

"Yeah, but don't worry about anything. He'll come around."

Madison chose not to respond to Steve's assertion, not wishing to dampen her mood by discussing his opinion-ated parents.

"So have you got big plans today?" she asked instead.

"No. I was thinking about just hanging out. I might go down to the club and see if I can't get in on a game of rac-quetball perhaps. Eventually, I'll head up to my parents' house to check in with my mother. Other than that, I don't know what to do with myself anymore," Steve said. "Thanks to you," he added.

"Why thanks to me?"

"Well, in comparison to the last few weeks that I passed with you, nothing else interests me. I mean, I guess I could flip through the old Rolodex and find a female companion to spend a few hours with and help ease my stress. What do you think of that idea?"

She could almost see Steve's devilish grin through the phone lines as he said this.

"I think that you are cruising for a fat lip, buddy, that's what I think," Madison barked.

"Baby, I'm going to go crazy here if I can't see you soon."

"So when can you come back?" Madison asked eagerly.

She was already beginning to feel that her own sanity would be stretched to the limits as she thought about the many miles that lay between them.

"I don't know. On Monday I'm scheduled to begin spearheading a series of meetings with a small, London-based mineral manufacturing company that we're taking on. There'll be so much to do with that, and I doubt that I'll be able to get away before that deal is completely settled and those folks have been brought on board. It could be weeks, maybe even a month or two."

"Are you serious? Well, I guess that's part of being a big-time executive, huh?"

"Something like that. What about you? What are you going to be doing?"

"When do you mean? Today?" Madison asked.

"Today, tomorrow and next week, too. I want to know what you're going to be up to every second that we're apart. That way I can just look up at my clock and picture you at some task or another."

"Oh, are you trying to keep tabs on me already, Mr. Elliott?" Madison teased.

"Yes, my lass, I am. Had I been thinking ahead, I might have purchased one of those electronic monitoring devices before I left the States. I could have hooked it around your little wrist and then I could monitor your every move," Steve said with mock seriousness.

"Stevenson Elliott, do you want me to come through this phone and slap the daylights out of you?" Madison asked, throwing one hand on her hip, her neck rolling in serious sister-girl attitude.

"Yes. Definitely. Yes…slap me, hard."

Madison burst out laughing at his silliness. They chatted for a while longer and by the time Madison announced that she needed to get going because she had an aerobics class to teach at the gym, they both felt comforted by their easy banter. This extended conversation would satiate them both, for the time being, but they also realized for the first time that a long-distance affair was not going to be the easiest challenge either of them had ever taken on. Madison cradled the phone to her chest for several minutes after the line had disconnected, wishing fiercely that it was Steve that she was holding close to her heart instead.

Steve's thoughts remained on Madison all day long. By the time he went to visit his mother, he was intoxicated by the sheer memory of her touch, taste and smell. His mother picked up on his obvious high spirits and after putting two and two together, determined that their sum was not the answer she was looking for. Never one to mince words, Janice hastened to address the situation before it went one step further. What she didn't know was that it had already gone further than even she could have surmised.

"Stevenson, now that you are back at home, I hope that you intend to put all *that* business behind you," she said.

"What business would you be referring to, Mother?" Steve asked.

"Come now, darling, I may be on the brink of old age, but I'm not so old that I don't know the signs. You are a young, handsome man and women are attracted to you, rightly so. All kinds of women. And I'm sure that you are attracted to them. However, acting on a physical or—" here Janice paused, searching for a tactful way to phrase what she felt she needed to say "—sexual attraction must not be mistaken for anything other than what it is. Do you follow me?"

"No, not really, Mother," Steve said with pretend coyness.

"Well, let me blunt. It is entirely acceptable for a man to act on his physical needs and animal magnetism. However, any woman who hastily gives away her chastity is not a woman with whom a man could possibly have a meaningful, long-term relationship. Let it go."

Janice's last statement was a demand that contained equal measures of intensity and insistence. A couple of days later, after expressing her disapproval over the various news reports of his tryst with *that Daniels woman,* as she put it, Janice Elliott had pretty much pushed the subject aside as if it were a nonissue. Steve's being one of England's most eligible bachelors, it seemed logical that the fact that Steve had been spied out on the town with a young American woman, with a reputation as a wildcat that preceded her, had been front page news on all of the English rags. Days after his return to England, the time he'd spent in New York with Madison was still a hot topic. The paparazzi here didn't waste any time cornering him outside of the office on his first day back to work, pummeling him with questions about Madison Daniels and his relationship to her. His resounding *no comment* did not satisfy them at all and he knew that he hadn't heard the last from them. In the meantime, however, he let sleeping dogs lie and as long as his parents seemed satisfied that things had returned to normal, he was content with keeping up the front. However, inside, his soul raged as he thought of Madison, wondering what she was doing and if she was thinking of him as much as he was thinking of her.

It did dawn on him that in light of the fact that Madison had had her share of love interests as the rags reported, there was the chance that he was dangling over the cliff of devotion all by himself. He wrestled with the idea that perhaps he had not meant nearly as much to Madison as she did to him, and maybe with time and distance between them, she would find it easy to move on. When such thoughts tortured him to the point of distraction, he picked up the telephone and called her, regardless of the time of day or night. The sound of her sweet voice, telling him how much she craved him and longed to be in his arms again, was enough to crush those demonic thoughts and fill him to the brim with infatuation.

Steve vacillated in and out of states of elation and despair in between working, and it was not long before the distress he was enduring became evident to his parents, particularly his mother. With a true mother's wit, as fallible as it might be at times, Janice surmised that the best thing for her son would be to spend time with a desirable young woman. She'd dismissed his affair with Madison as a frivolous *boys will be boys* type of escapade, grateful for the fact that the woman lived so far away. Of course, for her purposes, not just any woman would do. Genevieve Daltrey, the beautiful daughter of a member of British Parliament, became the chosen one. Genevieve was poised, beautiful, cultured and, most importantly, scandal-free. Janice orchestrated the meeting between Steve and Genevieve with the finesse of a seasoned matchmaker and manipulator.

The Elliotts hosted a dinner party at their six-acre estate on a clear summer evening. The guest list was a veritable who's who of England's elite. The caterer prepared a smorgasbord of delights for the thirty or so guests in attendance and as the expensive bubbly flowed and the caviar circulated, Steve watched as his parents did what they did best— held court. It was not a mistake when a striking woman was seated to his right. When his mother made the introductions, Steve could feel the intensity with which she spoke, as though he were a student being advised to pay close attention because she intended to test him later on.

"It's a pleasure to meet you, Ms. Daltrey," Steve said.

"Likewise, Mr. Elliott," she replied.

"Please, call me Steve."

"I will, if you'll call me Jenny." She smiled.

"Jenny. Is that short for Jennifer? Or how about Eugenia?"

Her laughter rang out in a high tinkle. "I'm afraid nothing as exotic as Eugenia. It's Genevieve. I was named after my grandmother."

"Genevieve. It sounds like the name of a queen. I like that. So tell me, how are you enjoying yourself so far this evening?" Steve asked politely.

"Your parents have a lovely home here. And the food, mmph, well, let's just say there goes my diet. Everything is marvelous."

"Yes, Mom and Dad do know how to throw an enviable affair. My mother is what you'd call a planner, and it does not matter how big or small the affair, she leaves no detail unperfected."

Steve chatted with Genevieve throughout all seven courses of the two-hour meal, which started with an appetizer and continued through soup, fish, entrée, meat, dessert and cheese. While he participated actively in the conversation, his mind was miles away. Afterward, he excused himself and headed off to find a quiet place to use the telephone. He called Madison at her apartment and then on her cell phone, receiving voice mail for both. He left a simple message that he was sorry he'd missed her and returned to the party, certain that if he stayed gone too long his mother would surely come searching for him. Indeed, when he slid into the living room, which had been rearranged to become a suitable ballroom complete with dancing space, a band and a bar, she appeared instantly at his side.

"There you are, dear. I was wondering where you'd made off to. Are you having a good time?"

"Yes, Mother. You've outdone yourself with this one," Steve said, kissing his mother's cheek.

"Thank you, sweetheart. Listen, I need to go over and chat with the VanKlines. Why don't you ask Genevieve to dance, dear. She's standing over there all by herself," Janice suggested, nodding discreetly across the room.

Steve followed his mother's gaze to the sultry figure positioned near the fireplace. A statuesque woman with long shapely legs and a tiny waist, Genevieve could easily pass for a runway fashion model. Her cinnamon skin was flawless and she wore her hair in dozens of tight curls piled high on top of her head. A couple of loose curls dangled around her temples, framing an angelic face, made up in reds and pinks that complemented the undertones of her unblemished face. The tee-length gown she wore had a fitted bodice speckled with silver stones, which accentuated a tight torso and generous cleavage, yet the full skirt gave her a youthful appearance. In black from head to toe, she definitely possessed an air of elegance and royalty.

Steve plucked a glass of champagne from one of the waiters' trays as he passed him by and in two large gulps had drained the glass. He deposited the glass on an empty table as he made his way across the room.

"Hello, again, Queen Jennifer Eugenia Daltrey. I trust that you're still enjoying yourself."

"Very much so. I was chatting with your mother a little while ago and she had quite a bit to say about you."

"Did she? Nothing too terrible, I hope," Steve stated.

"On the contrary. Your mother absolutely dotes on you. It would appear that you are something of a mama's boy," Genevieve remarked.

"Oh, now, that's not entirely true. But I am her only child so that might account for some of her fondness."

"Or it could be that you're just as much the sweet, loving son that she made you out to be. Don't be so quick to minimize a strong mother-to-son bond. Personally, I think it's cute."

"Oh, so I'm cute, huh…like a puppy? Well, Jenny, would you care to dance with me? I promise not to drool all over your shoes." Steve smiled.

"Since you've decided to get my name right at last, how can I refuse?"

Genevieve extended her hand and Steve guided them to the dance floor. With one arm around her waist and her hand resting in his, he held her firmly yet at a distance, a couple of inches separating their bodies. Gracefully tall and wearing high-heeled shoes, Genevieve was just about an inch shorter than Steve. They danced in that manner for a few songs until the band switched to an up-tempo number. Steve grabbed Genevieve's hands in his and began to hustle. He was quite talented on his feet, moving about with a style that he'd perfected after years of watching American dance videos. Genevieve could not help being impressed by the man who, in person, was as charming and engaging as she had been told he was.

They passed the evening laughing, chatting and dancing. For Steve, it was a nice distraction from his aching heart, yet when it was over, it was all but forgotten for him. He walked Genevieve out front to the valet parking attendants hired for the evening, saw her to her vehicle and shook hands warmly, wishing her a good night. He did not notice the approving smile his mother shot toward Genevieve when his back was turned, keeping him oblivious of the plans that had been hatched without his knowledge.

The moment he secured himself in his own vehicle to head back to his lonely apartment, Steve dialed Madison's numbers again. Once again, her melodic voice greeted him, appealing to him to leave a message. He hung up without doing so this time, his disappointment at not being able to speak with her directly lingering in the cool night air. Steve did not know how much more he could take of this separation and wondered if they even had a chance at a future together.

## Chapter 13

"I can't believe I let you talk me in to coming out here. I mean, there is no running water, no electricity and what the hell is that smell?" Madison complained, holding four of her fingers in front of her wrinkled nose.

"Madison, would you please stop complaining. It's high time you stopped being so damned bourgeois and embraced nature. What would you do if suddenly all of the conveniences of the world were gone? I mean, jeez, could you even survive?" Liza responded testily.

From the moment they'd loaded their gear into her Range Rover and got on the highway, Liza Penning had been re-thinking her decision to invite Madison up to the Adirondacks for the weekend. Madison had done nothing but complain about everything from the long ride to the musical selections that Liza played once they lost the FM radio stations.

If Madison had not been one of Liza's best friends, she probably would have pushed her out of the vehicle without stopping first. After the Daniels sisters and Liza had entertained their summer camp compadres with a knock-down-drag-out, Ali vs. Frazier fight, Madison and Liza had become best friends. Over the years they'd had their share of disagreements, but there was something about each of their natures that complemented the another, and where Madison was delicate and fussy, Liza was laid-back and unrefined. She had reached marginal success as a stand-up comic, landing bit roles on television comedy series and enjoying a comfortable lifestyle. Like Madison, she had come into her twenties kicking and screaming with her heels up, enjoying the advantages of coming from a privileged upbringing. When Madison relocated permanently to New York, Liza had thought that it would be great to have her partner in crime in the same city, which they could tear up together; however, Madison was steadfast in her vows to change her lifestyle and *grow up,* as she put it, causing a divide between them that was undeniable.

While she'd not entirely departed from her reckless ways, Liza, too, had become a little less irresponsible and rash in her behavior as she moved to the other side of twenty-five. Realizing that there was something to be said for maturing, she viewed the weekend as an opportunity for her and Madison to spend some time together contemplating their futures under the blanket of Mother Nature, secreted away from the temptations of the city. Now, however, she wasn't too certain that Madison wouldn't turn this into the trip from hell.

"What, pray tell, would be the point of surviving in a

dark world full of funky people?" Madison quipped as she examined the water well situated outside the log cabin.

As Liza retrieved their bags from the car, Madison surveyed the area, not very pleased with what she saw. The sun had begun to set and they were surrounded by dark thickets of trees and bushes on all sides. The whole scene was reminiscent of something out of a B-grade film of a slasher let loose at a campsite, and Madison felt sorely ill at ease. What Liza saw as tranquility and peace, Madison saw as vulnerability. She reached inside her Gucci tote, sifting around in it until she located her cell phone.

"Out of range?" she shouted with dismay when she could not get the phone to access a line. "Oh, you cannot be serious. I can't get a signal out here in the boondocks. Please tell me you've got a signal on your phone, Liza," Madison called out, her voice filled with panic.

"Nope. I don't even bother bringing my phone out here because it doesn't work."

"Well, in that case, I just know you have land service inside, right?" Madison asked, eyeing Liza suspiciously.

"Negative again. There's no landline. Look, Madison, the idea is to come out to the country and forget about the outside world. How could that work if you had the distraction of ringing telephones?"

Madison's grimace as she faced Liza was a mixture of disbelief and acute bewilderment. When she realized that her friend of almost two decades was entirely serious, Madison collapsed on the top of the four steps that led to the cabin's modest porch and held her head in her hands. Liza removed her digital camera from the breast pocket of the cargo vest she was wearing and snapped a few shots of

Madison. An amateur photographer, Liza would never be found without at least one camera nearby and at the ready, and normally Madison, an extrovert by nature, would pose for her without hesitation. This was a rare exception and when Liza realized that Madison was not in the mood to play model, she dropped the duffel bag she was holding and joined her friend on the stair, draping one of her thick arms around Madison's shoulders.

"Come on, Maddie. It's going to be fun. Did you know that the Adirondacks State Park stretches over more than six million acres, which makes it bigger than the Grand Canyon, Yosemite and Yellowstone all rolled up into one?"

When Madison shrugged her shoulders, Liza took that as an apparent sign that she was interested in the geography lesson and continued.

"The Adirondacks contain the only mountains in the eastern United States that are not Appalachian. There is so much space up here but comparatively hardly any people," Liza said excitedly.

"So?"

"So, that means you can walk for miles around this place without seeing another living soul. Trust me, when you've lived in New York for as long as I have, you'll come to appreciate a fact like that."

"Liza, I'm waiting for you to get to the part that is designed to make me feel better," Madison said testily.

"All right, how about this—I brought my George Foreman Grill and we can cook up some steaks—"

"I don't eat red meat anymore," Madison interjected in a deadpan tone.

"All right, well, I've got some chicken breasts and some

snapper. It'll be fun. We'll eat, and then sit back, paint our nails and read scary stories."

"Whoo-wee. Now, that sounds like a blast. Whatever was I thinking?" Madison asked dryly.

"Madison, can't you at least try to have a good time? I mean, seriously, what else would you be doing right now if you were at home?"

"Uh, how about taking a hot shower from my running faucet or, let's see, it is Thursday so I could be watching *Cold Case* or *E.R.* on my electric television. Ooh, I know…I could be using a light!"

"Look, it's getting dark. Now you can either sit out here sulking or you can help me get all this stuff inside. It's your choice."

Liza's no-nonsense tone was indicative of the fact that she had grown tired of Madison's disgruntled whining and was no longer planning to indulge her. Madison hated to rain on her friend's parade but she definitely was not feeling like much of a good Girl Scout.

"I'll take door number three, Monty…how about you drive me back to the nearest sign of civilization and I'll see if I can get a ride out of this godforsaken wilderness."

"Nope, that's not an option. You promised me that you were going to hang with me this weekend and that's what we're going to do, like it or not."

With that, Liza snatched up a few of their belongings, unlocked the door to the cabin and marched inside. Madison remained where she was, silently stewing while Liza made three trips back to the car until she'd retrieved the last of their things. The screen door banged shut behind her one last time, but Madison didn't budge. It wasn't until tiny gnats began swarming around her head and a mosquito sucked what felt like a liter of blood from her arm that she got up reluctantly and entered the cabin.

"What if Steve tries to call me? He'll be frantic," Madison pleaded as she plopped onto an ugly pea-green overstuffed sofa. She surveyed the room and, utterly dissatisfied by what she saw, threw her head back against the sofa and shut her eyes as tightly as she could manage.

"Since when do you make yourself so available to a guy? I thought that sitting by the phone, waiting for a man's call was not a part of your modus operandi. What gives?" Liza asked.

Madison opened her eyes and studied her friend. Liza was probably the closest person to Madison aside from Kennedy, but for the life of her Madison couldn't understand how they'd managed to remain so close over the years. They were complete opposites, rarely agreeing on anything, from clothes to environmental issues. Liza was a tall, fluffy size twelve on a good day. Her curly mane of hair was untamed and appeared to have a mind of its own. Where Madison believed in full body waxing, plucked eyebrows and black-mud soaks at day spas, Liza's favorite fragrance was Irish Spring and Listerine.

The one thing about Liza that Madison respected above all else was the fact that ever since they were kids, Liza had known what she wanted to do with the rest of her life. The stage was her passion and she worked hard to earn and maintain her place there. She was a dedicated performer and extremely focused when it came to her career. However, there was also another aspect of Liza that was equally as noticeable. Liza rarely dated and she was about as knowledgeable about men and relationships as she was about the different types of hair removal systems available. Talking to her about men was fruitless.

"I have never sat by the phone waiting for anyone's call, Liza. It just so happens that I enjoy talking to Steve and besides, I'd hate for him to waste a long-distance call talking to my voice mail."

"Mmm-hmm, right. How considerate of you," Liza remarked.

In an effort to put an end to the conversation, Madison decided to get up and help Liza unpack. Liza threw a couple of short logs from the pile situated near the door into the fireplace and lit a fire, which had the immediate effect of taking the chill off the cabin. Afterward, they made sandwiches and served themselves from the pints of potato and macaroni salad Liza had packed in the small Igloo she'd brought along. They ate, chatting aimlessly, and then Liza gave Madison a preview of her upcoming one-woman show that would be playing at the Chelsea Playhouse, a theater located off Broadway, in a couple of months. Once again, Madison realized how good her girl really was. A knock on the cabin door filled Madison with instant fear and she went for one of the iron pokers next to the fireplace, while Liza laughed at her cowardice.

"Hello," Liza said as she opened the door.

"Hello, miss. I'm Marcus Forster and this is my brother, Terrence. We, uh, we're staying in the cabin on the other side of the clearing."

"I see. Well, what can we do for you?" Liza asked.

Madison moved closer to the door so as to get a closer look

at the men. They were tall, well-built men, with light brown skin and heads shaved closely like men of the armed services.

"We noticed a lot of thick black smoke coming out of your chimney. You've probably got some sort of blockage," Terrence said.

Liza glanced over toward the fireplace.

"Really? We hadn't noticed," she said. "I mean, I don't really know much about fireplaces, but—"

"It's okay. You probably wouldn't know anything was wrong for a while…until the smoke starts to back up and come down the chimney and the cabin fills with smoke."

"Eww, that wouldn't be pretty," Liza said. "I guess we'll just put the fire out."

"Oh, great. What are we going to do for heat all night?" Madison asked.

Her tone of voice reminded Liza that this was just one more complaint for her to add to her list of reasons why they should pack up and head back to civilization.

"No need to do that. We could check it out for you," Marcus said.

"Oh, no. That's mighty nice of you guys, but we couldn't impose on you like that. I'm sure you must have other things to do," Liza said.

"Not really. While being up here in the woods away from all signs of human life is my brother's idea of a good time, I'm actually quite bored and we've only been alone here one day. Believe me, manual labor would be a welcome distraction at this point." Marcus smiled.

"Wow, I thought I was the only sane person left in this corner of the world. You are a man after my own heart. Please, come on in, fellows, and see what you can do because I refuse to be bored and frozen to death all in the same weekend," Madison quipped.

It turned out that Marcus and Terrence were both staff sergeants in the marines, native New Yorkers who had been stationed for the past six years at a base in Germany. Their main duties were as training officials, which helped them avoid seeing any action in Iraq. However, all that changed when Terrence decided that he wanted to go and assist his fellow servicemen overseas. Since a childhood pact made twenty years ago vowed that wherever one brother went, the other would follow, Marcus signed on for a tour of duty in Iraq with his brother. The duo was scheduled to depart in another month and had been given leave to spend time with their family and friends. Along with some high school friends, they'd rented the cabin for a couple of weeks of hiking, fishing and guy stuff. The party was just about over and everyone had gone home. The handsome brothers were now enjoying the last couple of days on their own to relax.

After the guys managed to clear the chimney, which turned out to be some broken branches that must have snapped from a tree during a storm and gotten wedged down in the structure, Liza was determined to repay them for their neighborly assistance. She prepared and served them dessert dishes of pound cake, whipped cream and fresh strawberries.

"How about a game of cards? Do you fellows play at all?" Liza asked, batting her eyes.

Madison tried not to appear nauseated at her friend's attempts at appearing coy, but it was quite difficult to pull it off.

"Do we play? Spades, Bid Whist, Tonk…pick your poison, girl, and prepare to get served. I'll have you know that we were the Westbrook High School cafeteria champs for four years running," Marcus boasted.

"Oh, shoot, I smell a challenge. Hope you boys brought your handkerchiefs to wipe away those tears when we finish spanking your butts, right, Maddie?" Liza said, her highly competitive nature coming out at the first sign of a contest.

Madison would much rather have called it a night, but she didn't want to appear ungrateful for their help. She dug the deck of cards out of Liza's game bag as instructed while Liza and Terrence assembled some chairs around a small card table they found in a closet.

"Okay, I think I've got a couple of hands in me, but I warn you guys, I'm getting a little sleepy," Madison stated, covering her mouth with one hand to stifle a yawn.

Thirty minutes later, it was quite obvious to both Madison and Marcus that at least two of them wanted to reduce the quartet to a duet. When Terrence announced that he and Liza were going to go for a walk, Madison simply raised an eyebrow and began packing up the cards. She watched as her friend walked out of the cabin, camera in tow, arm in arm with a man she hadn't known even existed a couple of hours before then, dangling a flashlight from her free hand. The flush of embarrassment she felt came from the knowledge that Liza was not doing anything that she herself hadn't done before, but somehow it seemed indecent now.

Madison yawned again, making it clear to Marcus that as far as she was concerned, the night was over.

"This was fun. Thanks for having us over…or should I

say allowing us to hang out once we barged in?" he joked at the door.

"Thank you for keeping us from burning the place down," Madison replied.

Madison locked the door behind him, hoping that Liza had had sense enough to take the keys with her. She wrapped a throw blanket over her body and lay on the sofa with the intention of reading for a while. However, before she knew it, the sun was rising and Liza was turning the key in the lock. Madison kept her eyes closed while her friend tiptoed past her into the bedroom, like an adolescent attempting to sneak in so that her parents don't realize she broke curfew. If it wasn't so ridiculous, Madison might have laughed out loud. By the time Liza emerged from the bedroom a couple of hours later, Madison had decided that she wouldn't say a word about it. If her friend wanted to sleep around, that was her business. With the press she had been getting lately, she appreciated that she was the last person in a position to judge someone else.

The weekend wasn't as bad as Madison had anticipated it being. She found herself enjoying Liza's company, although she was still slightly disturbed by her behavior with Terrence. Once they were alone again, however, they fell into a relaxed cadence with one another, sharing some personal truths that neither was really aware of before.

"Madison, tell me about this English guy you're so gaga over?" Liza requested.

Madison looked up from the crossword puzzle she'd been working on. Liza was stretched out in front of the fire reading through a script for a television series she was considering auditioning for. It was late Saturday evening and they'd enjoyed a quiet night alone after Liza refused Terrence's request to spend some more time together, an action for which Madison was quite proud of her girl. It was obvious that Liza was hot for the guy and he wasn't exactly avoiding catching what she was throwing his way.

At Liza's insistence, the four of them had spent part of the afternoon canoeing on a craft the guys had rented, and it turned out that Terrence was twice the enthusiastic tour guide that Liza was.

"Did you guys know that it was the Iroquois Indians who named the area *Adirondack,* which means *bark eater?* I don't really get the connection, but it's an interesting fact," Terrence said.

Madison looked quizzically toward Marcus, who simply shook his head from side to side, indicating that she shouldn't even bother to try to figure his brother out.

Terrence went on to explain that the lake they were currently paddling in was only one of the two thousand four hundred lakes and more than three thousand miles of river in the vast area. He also told them that the area boasted over two thousand mountain peaks, many of them rising well over three thousand feet, before Marcus told him to shut up. After her initial discomfort as the tight craft floated into the middle of the water, Madison relaxed and took in the sights, with Terrence providing intermittent commentary. Liza must have taken over one hundred photos of the lake, the mountains, other scenery and the four of them. After threatening to chuck the camera into the water, Madison did admit that the scenery was breathtaking and she was glad she'd come. She let her mind wander to what it would be like to paddle down that same lake with Steve, an idea that filled her with a secret pleasure.

"Are you mocking me again?" Madison asked suspiciously in response to Liza's present prying question.

"No, not at all. I'm serious. So far all you've told me is that you met at the dinner dance you went to with your parents. You went out on a few dates and then he left. There's got to be more to the story than that."

Madison agreed wholeheartedly. There was definitely a whole lot more to the story than those bare facts. Yet she was not sure how much she was ready to admit to Liza. It wasn't that she didn't trust her girl, because she did. She knew that a lot of people would sell out their own mother to the press for less than you could buy a steak dinner with, but she believed with all her heart that Liza was not that kind of person. Truth be told, Liza despised the tabloids and the media twice as much as Madison did. Her reluctance to talk came from the uncertainty she felt about her relationship with Steve. In fact, she was not even sure that what they had qualified as a relationship. It had all been so rushed, everything happening so fast and without warning that she was still reeling herself. And then he was gone, on a plane and back to his real life, and she was left here with the memories of their time together as minimal comfort. There were no guarantees in any situation, but this was even more precarious than most, given the distance between them and the other potential obstacles they faced.

"I don't know what to say, Liza. I'm really in to him. He's such a great person and we made this weird, instant connection," Madison said.

"Sounds like a movie."

"Something like that, but don't get it twisted…I know that real life is very different than those Hollywood tales. I guess you could say I'm taking it one day at a time and just waiting to see what happens." ·

"Okay, and that's the logical thing to do. Now, tell me what your heart says." Liza smirked.

Madison smiled, her answer written all over her face. Liza shook her head, happy that her friend had found someone that made her feel goofy, but worried for her all the same.

"Just be careful, girl. Don't let your heart make you act crazy," she warned.

Madison wanted to tell her that it was too late, but instead she just smiled, returning to her crossword puzzle where she'd drawn hearts with her and Steve's initials in the margin.

## Chapter 14

"I can't even picture you sitting around a campfire roasting marshmallows. Did she have to tie you up or hold you at gunpoint?" Steve laughed.

"What is this, mock Madison week? I'll have you know that I am quite the camper," Madison said.

She held her serious tone for all of two seconds before she burst out laughing at her own fib. By the time she finished telling Steve about her reaction when they first arrived at the cabin, he was in stitches. Hearing her talk and laugh reminded Steve of how much he missed her, underscoring the fact that maintaining a long-distance romance was not going to be easy.

"Steve, how are things going between you and your parents?" she asked.

Madison wanted to pretend that not only was the

distance between them a minor separation, but theirs was a blossoming relationship that was free from strife and complications. However, she was a realist and the reality was that on that first meeting it was clear that his parents didn't approve of her. What they'd gleaned from the scene with the reporter had given them a horrible first impression and she was not sure if the first impression would truly be a lasting one in this case. Then there was the matter of location—they lived in two different countries with two very different lifestyles. Not a day went by that she didn't chide herself for falling for a man who was virtually inaccessible. From the night she first shared coffee with Steve, she'd been thrown off balance.

"My parents are…difficult. I know that they just want what's best for me, but sometimes it's tough to align their wishes with my own," Steve replied.

Madison understood all too well what Steve meant. Yet, unlike her, Steve didn't seem ever to give his parents too much to disagree with.

"Steve, I've spent my adult life, and I guess you could say a good portion of my childhood, too, going against the grain and, more specifically, going against my parents. I grew up in the shadow of my sister Kennedy and for a long time I thought that I needed to be twice as bad as she was good in order just to have a voice. The more my parents tried to make me fit into their ideal of the perfect little Black American Princess, the more I resisted. But in the end, I realized that I was really only hurting myself."

"And making a name for yourself in the tabloids?" Steve asked tentatively.

They had not talked in detail about the night they'd met

or about their pasts. Although Steve wanted to know everything about her, her likes and dislikes, dreams and desires, he was unwilling to push her into telling him anything that she wasn't ready to talk about.

"Yeah, you know, when you're young and dumb, you don't really think about the fact that everything you do has consequences. I remember when I first left home to attend college."

"Where did you go to school?"

"Well, my parents wanted me to go Ivy League, like Kennedy did, but I didn't have the grades for it. My daddy was going to pull some strings with some of his cronies and get me in anyway, but I refused. I was going through my Black militant phase so I applied to Spelman. I was a little surprised when I actually got in, but I did. Anyway, I went to Atlanta and basically did everything in my power to piss my parents' money away. Two semesters later my grades were declining and I was headed toward academic probation. I decided that academia wasn't for me. I came back home, much to my parents' disappointment, and that's when things really got rocky between us."

Madison paused, reflecting on her words. It all seemed like such a long time ago when really, it was only a matter of a few years. At twenty-five years old, she was still able to look back on those days with clarity. The amazing difference, however, was the fact that she now possessed the ability to analyze her actions objectively and understand how much she'd grown since then.

"Looking back, I think my parents thought that if they gave me enough space and time, I'd eventually get it together. But I was a spoiled little girl who had too much freedom and disposable cash. Maybe all along I was waiting for them to pull the reins in and they were waiting for me to do the same for myself," she mused.

"Isn't that what you've done now?" Steve asked.

"Yes, but it took a long time for me to get where I am. I spent my early twenties partying around the clock, drinking way too much and getting involved with men who only wanted to use me. But don't get me wrong—I don't mean to sound like a victim, because I never did anything that I didn't want to do. I used men just as much as they used me. Older men will spend their money shamelessly in order to have a young pretty girl on their arm. Success translated into power in my mind and I attached myself to powerful men."

"When you say *men,* how many are you talking about?" Steve asked.

He couldn't help but feel a pang of jealous angst rising up in his chest. After all, he was a man and no man liked to think of his woman with another man, or men for that matter.

"I dated, Steve. It wasn't so much about quantity as it was about quality. I'm embarrassed to say that sometimes those men were married…. Sometimes they were just too damn old and the situations were inappropriate. I didn't care about commitment or fidelity. What does that do to you to hear me say that?" she asked.

If they were going to be open, Madison reasoned that all of the cards needed to be put out onto the table. She wanted everything Steve learned about her to come from her and not from what he read in the papers or heard from someone else.

"Honestly? It scares me a little. I mean, I'm no saint, either, but I do believe in monogamy. When I'm with a woman, I'm with her. The idea of her stepping out on me, or…or sleeping around, that's a tough one to swallow."

"I haven't met many guys who think like that, or women, either, for that matter. Then again, maybe it was just the type of people I used to surround myself with. I can say that I've decided that I don't ever again want to be anyone's good-time girl. I learned a lot during those years, about myself and my value as a woman, priceless lessons, so I can't sit here and tell you that I regret my past. What is certain is that now I am ashamed of the hurt and embarrassment I caused my family while I went through all those growing pains, as necessary as they were."

"I can respect that," Steve admitted.

"Thank you for saying that."

"You're welcome. Can I ask you a favor?"

"Sure."

"Can you promise me that you'll be faithful to me?"

Steve hated himself for needing reassurance, but his heart was too vulnerable not to seek it.

"I can promise you that I value myself and you too much to disrespect us. Fair enough?"

"Indeed, and I promise the same."

"So, here I am and here we are. I moved to New York earlier this year to learn how to stand on my own two feet. I promised myself that I would concentrate on me and stay away from anything that would distract me from that," she said.

"I guess I've sort of thrown a monkey wrench into that plan, huh?" Steve laughed.

"Sort of. Meeting you definitely wasn't in the plans."

"Do you regret it?" Steve asked, his voice tight with anticipation of her response.

"Not for one second," Madison said, meaning her words with all her heart.

"Good, because this is fate," Steve said.

"Is it really?"

"That's right. You and I were meant to meet and fall in love. It was written in the stars. As a matter of fact, I remember reading my horoscope a while back and it said you will meet a beautiful, sexy, woman, with a body like bam and a face like pow and she will be smart, independent and sassy!"

Madison laughed. "Your horoscope said all of that?"

"Definitely. I couldn't believe it myself, until I met you and I was like, wow! So now here we are and I'm trying to figure out how we can make this thing work because I can't really remember my life before you," Steve said.

"That's sweet, but—"

"No buts. I don't want to hear anything negative. I know what we're up against, but I also know how I feel about you. I admire the way you've gone out on your own, taking your life in your own hands. A lot of people would be content with spending their lives living off of Daddy's bank account and steering clear of responsibility."

"Shoot, responsibility is a little bit overrated, you know, and right now, Daddy is still helping me foot the bills. I've been thinking about going back to school, but whatever I do, it's going to be a while before I'm totally independent."

"That's okay. At least you're headed there."

Madison's heart swelled at the amount of confidence

Steve had in her. Although he hadn't known her very long, he'd been able to look inside and see her heart. He hadn't judged her from the outside like so many people do, but instead, was able to take her at her word and believe in what he saw in her.

"I want to see you," she said, suddenly overwhelmed by a need to have him in her arms again.

"I know how you feel. I'm right there, too," Steve lamented.

Steve tried to reassure her that it wouldn't be long before they had an opportunity to see each other again, even though he wasn't too sure about that fact himself. He knew that it was impossible for him to get away right now because his parents would put up all kinds of roadblocks and opposition to his returning to New York. He had to figure out a way to smooth things over with them and clear up his schedule because every night since the night he'd made love to Madison had been long and interminable. He needed her in his arms again more than he needed the air in his lungs. Until then, he had to hold on to the faith he had that she cared for him as much as he cared for her. It was that faith that helped him keep things in perspective, even when doubts tugged at his subconscious.

# Chapter 15

"Aah," Steve exclaimed as he hoisted Madison off of her feet and into his arms, swinging her around and around in the air.

"Steve, Steve…put me down. People are staring at us," Madison screeched, feigning embarrassment.

It was a fact that just laying eyes on Steve again was the equivalent of waking up as a child on Christmas morning to find the ground outside covered with freshly fallen snow and a brand-new puppy under the pine Christmas tree. She was certain that life did not get much better and was beside herself with glee.

"I don't care. Let them stare. Ooh, girl, I missed you so much."

Steve lowered Madison to her feet, only to encircle her body with his arms in a tight bear hug. She was equally dizzy from the spinning and from the excitement she felt in seeing him. Two months had felt like forever, solidifying for both of them the fact that the affair they'd begun back in New York City was far from being over. Indeed, they each knew that it could never be completely over in their hearts, no matter what happened between them.

Madison had so much to say to Steve, now that she was face-to-face with him, yet words escaped her as she felt his sturdy arms holding her as if she were his pillow during a sound sleep. At length, he drew back ever so slightly, looking into her face as if in that one look he could memorize every one of her features. Finally, he leaned his face toward hers, capturing her mouth with his. Suddenly, they were transported miles away from the boisterous travelers who surrounded them in the hectic airport, to a place where only they resided, lost in one another's embrace.

When she'd first received the FedEx package from Steve, she'd been giddy with delight. Inside the brown box had been a number of individually wrapped items, each of which brought an even bigger smile to her face.

First, there was a package marked number one. She pulled off the shiny gold wrapping paper to reveal a two-foot plush teddy bear with shiny brown eyes and a fluffy tan coat. The bear was wearing a red T-shirt with white lettering that read I Miss You This Much and the bear's arms were extended as wide as they could go.

The second package, also wrapped in the same shiny gold paper, was a Polaroid picture of Steve holding the teddy bear in one arm and a dozen red roses in the other. He was standing in front of the Silver Jubilee Bridge, looking as sexy as she remembered in a crisp white button-down shirt, black denim jeans and black loafers. His mouth was turned down in an exaggerated frown and he'd written the words *pathetic soul* across the bottom of the photograph.

The third and final article that she drew from the box was a white envelope. Inside was an open, round-trip airline ticket, first class, from Kennedy Airport to Manchester, England, in her name. She'd just about burst from the excitement, completely enamored by his thoughtfulness and the romantic nature of his gifts. She'd dialed him up immediately and after a brief conversation, because he was in a meeting, promised him that she'd book a flight for that very weekend.

In the days before her departure, she'd gone hot and cold at the prospect of seeing him again. While she was overjoyed at the thought of seeing, touching and smelling him, feeling his strong arms around her and hearing his voice live without the two-second delay of the telephone, she was also quite nervous. They had not talked much about his parents, but she did not get the sense that things were entirely smooth with them. She was wary of how they would receive her and while she had never been one to give a damn about what people had to say or thought about her, this was very different. These were people who meant a lot to someone who had come to mean a lot to her, and for the first time, the opinion of others did matter to her.

All of those concerns vanished the moment she found herself in Steve's arms again. It was a long while before they could part enough to proceed through the gates of Manchester airport and out into the rainy streets. Madison had spent the entire ride to Steve's loft with her face pressed against the passenger-side window like a puppy. Steve shouted out the names of streets and tourist attractions as they passed, giving her a succinct history of Manchester as he weaved expertly through the busy traffic. Madison pleaded with him to slow down to afford her a better view of the sights, but Steve was struggling with his own desire that was creating an urgency within him to get her back to his place as quickly as possible.

"So tell me more about what it is that you and your father do over there at the Elliott Corporation," Madison said.

"I don't know how good a bedtime story this makes, but I'll see if I can't spice it up a bit," Steve said, settling his head across Madison's thighs.

They had spent their first four hours together reacquainting themselves within the walls of Steve's trendy loft. Making love to say hello was twice as mind-blowing as it had been when they were saying goodbye.

Steve's place was a typical bachelor's pad, sparsely but tastefully furnished. His bed was large and covered with simple powder blue cotton sheets. A plasma television hung on the wall directly in front of the bed, equipped with a surround-sound system. A bureau and treadmill were the only other furnishings in the room. On top of the bureau was a picture of Madison taken last year on a beach in Aruba. Her hair was long and relaxed back then and the green bikini she wore left little to the imagination. Steve had taken the photo out of an album he'd leafed through at Madison's apartment, despite her protests that he find one a little more modest. She hoped his parents never saw that photograph, because that would surely be the final nail in her coffin as far as they were concerned. Steve showed her his most prized possession, which he had never shown anyone else. He kept a small jewelry box in one of his drawers. In it was a small brass medal.

"This belonged to my grandfather. He'd belonged to the infantry regiment of the Jamaica Defence Force when he was a young man and he won this for showing bravery. He gave it to me before I left Jamaica," he explained.

His expression alone showed her how deeply he continued to feel the pain of losing his grandparents, and she was honored that he felt close enough to her to share it with her.

Nestled in Steve's bed, a cool breeze from the ceiling fan blowing across their nude bodies, Steve accepted the spoonful of French vanilla ice cream Madison offered as he prepared to tell her his family's story of success.

"Let's see, well, in 1952 Reynolds Metals began producing bauxite for commercial use. Bauxite is one of the world's best natural resources and one of the cheapest to manufacture. A few years after that, the island became the largest producer of bauxite in the whole world, which is amazing for a tiny island like Jamaica. After dropping out of school at around fifteen, my father had spent his early years working at the Nain plant in St. Elizabeth for Alumina Partners of Jamaica. Even though tourism became the biggest source of income for the island by the early eighties, mining was still a huge deal…an important part of the economy for the export income it produced. My father realized early on that if he wanted to really capitalize off of the market, he was going to have to make it out of the mines and into the corporate offices. He didn't have any formal training, but he knew the earth and he was shrewd…a very lethal combination," Steve reported proudly.

"Ah, a self-made man, huh?"

"Yep. When we moved to England he'd accepted a position with Reynolds Metals. He stayed there for a few years, moving up in the ranks, and when the time was right, he struck out on his own."

"And he's been shooting upward like an arrow ever since?"

"Like a flaming rocket," Steve said.

"Where do you fit into the scheme?"

"You know, Madison, I really don't know. I used to know exactly what I wanted out of life. But I don't know, somewhere between fifth and seventh grade, things got a little fuzzy," Steve said.

Madison tapped the top of his forehead lightly.

"Stop being silly," she scolded.

"I'm serious, babe. I went from being a totally focused kid, an exact replica of my dad, to a flighty thrill-seeker who travels abroad and falls in love with short foreigners."

"That's it," Madison shouted, pushing Steve's head from her lap and pouncing on top of him.

They wrestled and laughed for a while before their games ignited their passion and they spent the remainder of the night making up for all the time they'd lost.

Steve took the next few days off from work, and to Madison's delight, he treated her to an all-out, no-holds-barred tour of England. Their days were spent sightseeing and shopping and their nights were filled with romance and passion. She'd traveled a good deal in her lifetime and, with her family, had been exposed to some of the most magnificent visuals the world had to offer. However, seeing the country with Steve by her side made it all brand-new for her and she felt privileged by the opportunity to get to know his homeland through his eyes.

As Liverpool was the home of The Beatles and other famous pop bands of the sixties, Madison was eager to tour this center of youth culture. Steve's father had a company apartment in Liverpool, which Steve used occasionally when he worked late as it was within walking distance to the office. They spent a few days there while Steve showed her everything of interest he could think of in his country. Steve, an avid English football fan, was borderline fanatical about introducing Madison to the sport. He took her to a game at Anfield to watch his favorite club, Liverpool F.C., which was the most successful team in Britain, and the 2006 holder of the European Cup.

They spent an afternoon at the Aintree Racecourse, which was to the north of Liverpool in Sefton—home to the Grand National, one of the most famous events in international horse racing. Madison placed her first ever horse bet, delighted like a schoolgirl when her horse crossed the line in third place, even though she'd lost.

They also attended a hilarious play at the Liverpool Playhouse and then had dinner at a trendy jazz club and restaurant in the area. Steve preferred to keep Madison to himself as much as possible, turning down numerous offers for double dates from his friends. On their own, the lovers spent nights walking along the waterfront, enjoying the spectacular view of Liverpool's skyline. From there she was able to take photographs of some of the most impressive buildings, including the Royal Liver Building, the Cunard Building and the Port of Liverpool Building, structures known as the Three Graces as they are the most memorable images of Liverpool's dynamic architecture. During each day, while Steve ran into the office for a couple of hours, Madison either slept in or strolled the neighborhood on her own. A week passed before she even broached the subject of his parents, but they both knew that it was an inevitable topic.

## Chapter 16

"That's precisely why I didn't tell you that Madison was coming to visit me, Mother. I knew you would have a coronary, and I didn't want to hear it. Now, she's here and I'd like you to meet her."

"No, thank you," Janice said hotly.

She studied her son's face, wondering who this man standing before her was. It was certainly not the obedient son she'd raised, as he was now making demands on her.

"Mother, I can't believe you are acting like this."

"Like what, Stevenson? How do you expect me to act when you come here demanding that I entertain some floozy you met while on vacation and have the audacity to bring her to our home. Your father and I were adamant in our request that you break things off with her, and you have defied us."

"Mother, do you hear yourself? You're acting like I'm six years old and you've caught me coloring on my bedroom walls with permanent markers again. I'm a grown man, Mother."

"That's one way of describing yourself. Yet, Mr. Grown Man, tell me why you snuck behind our backs and brought this girl here instead of being up front with us. You never used to do things like that."

Steve shook his head gravely, feeling as if he was waging a battle in a war that had already been lost. Janice moved toward her dressing table, opening the top drawer. She retrieved two magazines from inside and thrust them toward her son.

"Come on, Mother. I'm not interested in anything those rags have to say. I can't believe you would fall for even half of what is written in those things."

"I'm curious to know, Stevenson, how much your friend has told you about herself. She's uneducated and even has a criminal record. Did you know that?"

Steve took the magazines from his mother, tossing them on the king-sized four-poster bed she shared with his father.

"A criminal record? Oh, Mother, stop exaggerating. She and some friends got snagged for disorderly conduct outside a bar in Aruba last year. Not exactly what you could call criminal activity, Mother. Look, Madison and I have laid all of our cards on the table and, frankly, I don't care about anything those magazines or anyone else has to say about her. She dropped out of college because that scene just wasn't for her. That doesn't make her uneducated. What she may lack in formal training she definitely has

learned in experience. She's a world traveler, she comes
from a hardworking family and what's more, she is a caring
and genuine individual."

"You barely know her," Janice replied.

"I'm not asking for you to throw her a party. I'm asking
for you to not act like a close-minded bigot who relies on
gossip rags to give her character analyses on people.
Surely, I thought that you had your own mind," Steve said.

Janice's slap across Steve's face was weak and unmoti-
vated. She had never raised a hand against her son in all of
his twenty-seven years and even though he had angered her
beyond all sensibilities, she could not make herself strike
him with any semblance of force or conviction.

Steve grasped his mother's hand in his, withdrawing it
from his face.

"Mom, please. Just meet her. Can't you do that for me?
Just spend a few minutes talking to her and getting to know
her and you'll see that all of that stuff you've heard is a
bunch of bull. She is a beautiful person…her spirit and her
mind. Those are the things that matter, aren't they? People
make mistakes, Mother. Sometimes they are big ones and
sometimes they are miniscule. Madison has not done
anything in her life that is so insurmountable and unfor-
givable that she deserves to be shunned. She is a good
person with a big heart and…and I love her, Mother."

Janice's eyes grew wide at the sincerity in her son's
voice. "Steve—"

"I love her," Steve said resolutely.

Janice sighed, knowing that she could not refuse her son
no matter how much she was against his involvement with
Madison. She nodded her head in solemn resignation.

"Fine. I'll meet her. We'll have lunch tomorrow, here at the house. Bring her out at noon."

"Thank you, Mother."

"Do not thank me. I have not changed my mind in the least. I will meet the girl and I will be cordial to her. I can't promise you any more than that."

"I understand," Steve said, preparing to leave. "Listen, I need to run. I've got to pick Madison up from the spa at the Lowry Hotel. See you tomorrow?"

Janice nodded. "Stevenson, one more thing. I won't mention any of this business to your father just yet. He's got a lot on his plate right now, and I won't add one more morsel. Understood?"

Steve nodded. He was pleased with the progress he'd made with her and was not about to push his luck by trying to bring his father on board at the same time.

"Relax," Steve said, squeezing Madison's sweaty palm.

"I can't help it. I'm usually not at all nervous meeting people, but your parents and I didn't exactly get off to a stellar start."

"Thank you, James," Steve said to the family butler as he showed them into the sunroom where lunch had been set out in anticipation of their arrival.

"Good luck," James whispered to Steve as he left them alone.

Steve understood from James's conspiratorial tone that everyone in the house had already gotten an earful from his mother about today's luncheon. He swallowed hard, refusing to show any signs of discomfort to Madison, who was already on edge. He watched as she tucked a loose lock behind her ear. He brushed the side of her cheek with his free hand.

"You look beautiful," he said, meaning it with the utmost sincerity.

Every time he looked at her, Steve was taken aback at how naturally stunning she was. Her hair had grown longer since he'd met her in New York and now her honey-colored locks hung down to her earlobes. Her skin was fresh and glowing, accented by a light dusting of bronze facial powder and earth-toned eye shadow, and her succulent lips were finished with a frosted cinnamon lipstick. The simple short-sleeved, turquoise-and-white sundress she wore was one of the outfits she had picked up when they'd shopped in Lancaster and it flattered her shapely figure tremendously. Steve was just about to give in to the overwhelming urge to kiss her when his mother stepped into the room.

"Well, Stevenson. I was beginning to think I'd gotten the time wrong," she said.

Janice Elliott was dressed in all black, a sleeveless turtleneck sweater and black rayon slacks. Her hair was pinned away from her face, which highlighted her high forehead and severe features. She looked as though she were headed to a funeral or a court appointment instead of a lunch date on her own property.

"Good afternoon, Mother," Steve said.

He didn't bother to remark that it was only five minutes after twelve, their scheduled meeting time. He released Madison's hand and approached his mother, giving her a quick peck on the cheek. "Mother, I'd like you to meet Madison Daniels, once again. Madison, this is my mother, Janice Elliott."

"A pleasure, Mrs. Elliott," Madison said, extending her hand to the stern-looking woman.

Janice shook Madison's hand briefly.

"Have a seat, dear," Janice said to Madison.

Steve pulled out a chair for his mother first and then, on the opposite side of the iron-and-glass table, did the same for Madison. He sat at the center of the table, between the two women. Janice picked up a crystal pitcher of lemonade and poured a glass for herself, handing the drink over to Steve when she'd finished.

"So, Ms. Daniels, how was your flight?"

"Please, Mrs. Elliott, call me Madison. The flight was long but comfortable. They actually served a really nice salmon dinner."

"Oh, I absolutely despise airplane food. I'd rather starve than eat anything on those flights," Janice scoffed.

Madison glanced at Steve, who raised his eyebrows and grinned at her, touching her hand lightly across the table.

"Mom, did I tell you that Madison's father is a plastic surgeon? He's got a pretty famous clientele," Steve said before turning to Madison. "My mother likes to look at celebrity photographs and guess who's had what type of work done and assess the good jobs from the bad. She's pretty good at spotting the signs of recent alterations."

"With all the people out there in the world who are dying to be something they aren't, I'm sure your father has quite a booming practice," Janice said.

"Yes, Dad does all right. He loves his work and he's very respected in the medical community for what he does," Madison said proudly.

"It's just such a shame that many of these doctors don't

care enough about their patients to say when enough is enough. I mean, if there weren't so many doctors who were willing to take people's money, perhaps they wouldn't let people who already look like plastic mannequins go under the knife anymore."

"I agree. That's one thing my dad is very strict about. If a patient can't produce a complete medical history and records from all prior surgeries, he won't even agree to a consultation. One time he told me about a woman who'd come to see him. She'd had so many nose jobs that her nose was about to collapse and she still wasn't satisfied. Not only did he refuse to do the surgery, but he convinced the woman to see a colleague of his who is a psychiatrist. To this day the woman still sends him a Christmas card every year, thanking him for intervening."

"That's something. I guess your father is one of the good guys then," Janice said.

Madison simply nodded, unable to tell if she was being sarcastic or not. There was something unreadable in Janice Elliott's clipped manner of speaking and reserved attitude that made it difficult for Madison to figure her out.

"Mrs. Elliott, lunch was absolutely magnificent. Thank you for having me over," Madison said.

"Yes, it was quite lovely," Janice said. "I must remember to tell Martha, the cook, that you enjoyed her fare. So tell me, Madison, when will you be heading home? I'm sure you must have a job or some other pressing business to tend to."

"Um…well, I haven't really decided just yet. But you're right, I do need to get back soon," Madison said, her back stiffening.

It was obvious to her that Mrs. Elliott was making some sort of indirect statement about her leaving. It didn't take a rocket scientist to figure out that the lady was being as cordial as she could find it within herself to be, for Steve's sake, and that she wouldn't lose a wink of sleep once Madison was back on a plane and headed far away from her son. At that point, Madison decided that it was no use going out of her way to be amiable to Steve's parents. They had made up their minds about Madison and nothing she could say or do would change that. For his sake, however, she continued to smile, thanked Mrs. Elliott again for having her over and left with her head held high and her disappointment in check.

## *Chapter 17*

"So this is the lovely young lady who's got my boy spinning in circles these days. I'm very glad to make your acquaintance, Madison, and do you by chance have a sister?" Neil said, kissing the back of Madison's hand gallantly.

Cornelius Oliver Wesley was Steve's best friend since they had shared a dorm room their freshman year in college. The end of Madison's two-week stay in England was approaching quickly and Neil had basically threatened bodily harm to Steve if he didn't bring her around to have dinner with him and the rest of their close-knit circle of friends.

Neil, as he was affectionately known, was on the short side for a man, just a couple of inches taller than Madison. He had reddish undertones to his light brown skin and dazzling hazel eyes. A slim build and manicured hands completed the picture. He was what women would call a pretty boy, with a thousand-watt smile and charm to match.

Madison smiled at Neil, while Steve protectively placed an arm around her shoulders.

"All right now, I already warned you to behave yourself tonight, man," Steve said.

"Neil, it's so nice to finally meet you. Steve has told me a lot about you," Madison said.

"Don't believe a word of what this joker has to say," Neil said. "Come on in."

He showed them in to his metropolitan flat, leaving the door ajar after them.

"Ted and Nina should be coming up right behind you guys," Neil said.

He ushered them into the foyer of his place, Madison first, followed by Steve and then Neil brought up the rear.

"Let me give you a tour of my swinging bachelor's pad. Whoo-wee, if these walls could talk," Neil said, stepping around Steve and taking Madison by the arm.

She followed him down a short hallway, her rubber soles squeaking on the highly waxed hardwood.

"First is the kitchen. In here, I whip up tantalizing dishes that keep the ladies coming back for more. I must say I really outdid myself today. Wait until you get a whiff of this."

Neil lifted the lid off of a Crock-Pot, waving it in front of Madison's nose.

"Mmm, smells good. What is it?" she asked.

"Ahh, you'll see. It'll knock your socks off. Might even make you dump my 'no cooking' best friend back there and take up with me," Neil teased.

He led her around the rest of the apartment, which was

oddly shaped in a circular fashion. They ended up back near the front door, where they entered a room to the left that turned out to be the living room. Already seated in the spacious room were Steve, three men and two women.

"There you two are. I was about to come and find you. Thought I was going to have to knock this one out," Steve said, taking a playful jab at Neil.

He kissed Madison on the cheek.

"All right, so let me make the introductions. Over there you've got Tommy and Arman. We went to grade school together, believe it or not," Steve said.

"True story—I used to beat your boy up every day during first grade and take his Twinkie at lunchtime," Arman laughed.

"Shut up, man. Seated at the piano is Jasmine, our resident musical genius. She plays the viola in the BBC Concert Orchestra."

"Hey, Madison. Love your locks." Jasmine smiled.

Madison returned the compliment with a smile and a quick nod of her head.

"On the sofa this is my main man, Ralph. He works with me…in finance. And last, but not least, is Jordanne, Arman's wife. For the life of us we still can't figure out what she sees in him," Steve joked.

"Well, it's a joy to meet all of you. And, Neil, you have a lovely home. It's got a woman's touch to it."

"Oh, no, don't tell him that. He already thinks of this place as a chick magnet," Ralph laughed.

"Jealousy is a sickness, Ralph, my buddy. I can't help it if my home is a love lair, desire den, pleasure palace—"

"Enough!" both Ralph and Steve shouted in unison.

"Keep it up and Arman won't be allowed to come back into this freaky little place," Jordanne warned.

Arman glared at Ralph.

The final pair joining them, Ted and Nina, arrived at that point and Neil made the introductions. The evening was full of good-natured fun. The meal Neil had prepared, a mixed seafood stew, angel-hair pasta and fluffy, freshly baked biscuits, was magnificent and it went well with the wine Jordanne and Arman had brought.

Afterward, over coffee and key lime cheesecake, they played a rousing round of Trivial Pursuit in which Ted and Nina racked up the couple's high score.

"So, Madison, Steve tells us that you guys met at one of those stuffy political functions?" Neil asked.

"Actually, it wasn't that stuffy. It was nice," Madison said, her eyes meeting Steve's, who leaned over and kissed the spot above her left eyebrow.

"Gosh, you two are way too mushy. I'd bet if you'd met in the middle of a mosquito-filled swamp, you'd say the same thing," Neil kidded.

"Well, it was just a really, really great night," Steve said. "Don't hate."

"I bet it was great…right up until the paparazzi showed up," Ralph said.

Neil, who was sitting closest to Ralph, kicked him beneath the table as discreetly as possible. Everyone else grew silent, averting their eyes from Madison. The room was suddenly filled with an embarrassed tension as thick as the cheesecake Neil had served for dessert.

"Are you kidding? That was the best part of the whole night!" Madison quipped, not missing a beat.

"Seriously?" Ralph asked.

This time Neil slapped Ralph upside his head.

"What do you keep hitting me for?" Ralph barked.

"Because you're an ass, that's why," Jordanne said. "Madison, excuse our friend. Prudence is definitely not his strong suit."

"It's okay, Jordanne, really. I know you guys have read some awful things about me, but trust me, I'm not the gold-digging piranha the press paints me out to be," Madison said, her comment tinged with a lightheartedness designed to put everyone back at ease.

"Please. We all know that you can't believe one-eighth of what those jerks print in their trashy rags," Nina stated. "I can't imagine having them in your business all the time, chasing you around like a dog in search of a bone."

Throughout the remainder of the evening, which was short-lived after that point, Madison noticed how quiet Steve had grown. It was obvious to her that he was disturbed by his friends' comments and the moment they were alone in his car, she asked him about it.

"What's the matter with you?" she asked.

"Nothing. I'm just tired," Steve said without looking at her.

He ran his hand across his head, staring out at the road ahead of him. A tight line formed at his mouth and his brow was wrinkled in concentration. Madison chewed her bottom lip for a moment, feeling her own heat rising inside. She contemplated her next words carefully, choosing her next statement with caution.

"Do you want to talk about it or are you going to sulk all night long?" she asked.

"Talk about what? There's nothing to talk about."

"Steve, don't do this."

"Don't do what?"

Steve glanced at Madison, his gaze holding her eyes briefly before turning away. The nonchalance he was attempting to display in his words was proven false by the fiery look in his eyes.

"This. I'm not going to play this 'let's just sweep it under the rug and it'll go away' game with you. That's not my style."

"Not your style, huh? So what is your style, Madison?"

"Pull the car over, Steve," Madison said firmly.

"Come on—"

"Pull the damned car over, please," she repeated more forcefully.

Steve glanced in his mirror, driving another few meters until he could safely maneuver to the side of the road. He eased the car to a stop, shifted into Park and leaned back in his seat.

"So apparently I've been the topic of some conversation amongst your friends. Tell me exactly what part of that pisses you off the most?" Madison said, her eyes boring into Steve.

"Madison, this is ridiculous. I really don't see what you have to be so angry about."

"Look at me, Steve."

Steve turned to face Madison. His heart lurched as he looked at her, conflicted between his anger and wanting to just pull her into his arms.

"Talk to me…please?" she pleaded.

"I just can't help wondering if it's always going to be like this. Is everyone always going to think the worst of you? Is your name going to constantly be slung through the mud? Madison, I just don't know if I can deal with this. I can't fight everyone."

"I don't need you to fight people for me, Steve. All I need is for you to love me. People are going to talk whether there is something to talk about or not, Steve."

"Madison, don't talk to me like I'm a stupid little kid. I know that. I'm not caught up in what people say, but damn, it's not just people. You're talking about my friends, my colleagues, my family. It's…" Steve slapped the palm of his hand against the steering wheel, his frustration stealing his words.

"Steve, what is this really about?" Madison asked.

She reached across the car and placed her hand over his on the steering wheel. Steve studied her hand, the contrast of her light skin against his brown, her smallness against his largeness. He wanted to always feel her next to him, with him, and it killed him to even consider the alternative possibility.

"My mother and I had a disagreement…after we had lunch with her the other day," Steve said.

He hung his head.

"About me," Madison stated, her words lacking the inflection of a question.

"She said some things, some nasty things, and then I said a bunch of stuff, equally as nasty. Madison, I've never seen her act like this before, and I just don't know how to handle it."

Madison almost felt sorry for him. His anguish was obvious to her. Yet all the same, she could not feel for him any worse than she was feeling for herself.

"You know something, Steve? You've got a lot of nerve. You expect me to sit here and console you because, what, poor little Stevie just got smacked on the fanny by Mommy for being a bad boy? Give me a break. Maybe if you stop trying to be a perfect little robot and do what you know is right for you, you wouldn't be so torn up!"

Madison's voice was raised now. She snatched her hand away from Steve, folded her arms across her chest and looked out of the window. It had begun to drizzle, providing a gloomy backdrop to their dismal saga.

"Everybody can't be like you, Madison. Some people actually give a damn about what their families want for them…what other people think of them. Sorry that I'm not a bad-ass rebel like you are."

Steve's anger flashed hotly, matching Madison's.

"I'm not asking you to be a rebel," Madison said after a brief silence.

"What are you asking me?"

Steve's voice had lowered a few decibels, as had Madison's.

"Steve, if you want this relationship to work, if you really want us to be together, then you're going to have to tune out everything and everyone else and focus on us."

"That's easier said than done, Madison."

Steve turned to face her finally. His eyes were soft as he studied her face. He reached over, taking her tiny hand in his and squeezing it tightly.

"Do you love me?" she asked.

"Yes. Yes, I love you, Madison," Steve said with conviction and without the slightest moment of hesitation.

"Then believe in that, Steve, like I do. No matter what people have to say about us, you've got to trust in me."

"I want to," Steve said.

"Then do it, Steve. Do it or this is never going to work."

Steve leaned toward Madison and she moved to meet him halfway. They opened their arms to each other, their embrace yielding. Neither of them spoke anymore about the situation that night, a fragile peace having settled between them. A few days later, when Steve took Madison to the airport for her return flight to the United States, all of his doubts and concerns lingered as he kissed her goodbye. And as she boarded the plane, she, too, carried misgivings about their future. Yet one thing was certain for both of them and that was the love they felt for each other.

## Chapter 18

Madison walked along the outskirts of the park, Brandy trotting at her side with her tongue hanging out of her mouth and her tail wagging. They'd been walking for over an hour as Madison tried to clear her mind. She'd been back in New York for two weeks and the more time passed, the more she realized that she wanted to be with Steve. This bi-continental relationship would not suffice for much longer, of that she was certain. She also knew that he could not, at this point in his life, relocate permanently to the United States. The only logical solution would be for her to move to England with him; however, that answer only opened up a whole other basket of questions. For starters, would he even want her to come?

She could not deny the fact that the ridiculous notoriety thrust upon her by the media created a prickly blockage

between them. Steve had his family and friends to contend
with and as much as she would like to believe that he
should be able to just deal with it, another part of her
realized that it was not an easy thing to do. It didn't matter
that half of what had been printed about her wasn't true and
the other half was an embellishment of the truth. Nor did
it matter that all of it was her private business that had no
*business* being smeared across the pages of anyone's pub-
lication. Everything had become so complicated so
quickly, and as she meandered through Central Park, she
prayed for a solution that would clear the way for her and
Steve to just love each other.

"Excuse me, miss?" a voice called from behind.

Madison turned around to find a tall handsome man
towering above her. He was wearing a white sleeveless
workout shirt, light gray nylon jogging pants and white
sneakers.

"Uh, your dog looks like she could use a little water,"
he said.

"What?" Madison asked.

She looked from the man's face down to Brandy, who at
that moment she'd forgotten was even beside her. The poor
dog was panting heavily and had stretched out on the ground
between them as if saying that she didn't care if the apoca-
lypse was coming, she was not about to take another step.

"Oh…oh, I guess we've been walking for a long time.
I'm sorry, girl," she said, stooping down to stroke the side
of Brandy's neck and shoulder.

"I believe there's a dog-watering station just around that
bend over there," he said, pointing east from where they
stood.

"Yes, I think you're right. Uh, thank you," Madison said, rising to stand erect again.

"So, this pretty girl here is Brandy and you are…?" he asked.

The man was fine. There was no denying that. He was smiling at her, a full-lipped, pearly-white smile that she surmised had probably caused many a knee to buckle.

"Madison," she replied.

"Madison. It's nice to meet you. I'm Maxwell," he said, extending his hand.

*You certainly are,* is what she thought to herself. Instead she shook his hand and said, "Likewise."

"Would you mind if I walked with you to get Brandy here saturated? I was headed that way anyway," Maxwell said.

"What are you, some type of dog guardian who scours the park looking for canines in distress?" Madison joked.

"Yep, how'd you know? I mean, I don't have my cape on today," Maxwell laughed.

Madison tugged at Brandy's leash and the dog responded, and jumped to her feet. They strolled slowly across the grass toward the dog-watering station.

"So how old is Brandy here? About six or seven?" Maxwell asked.

"She's actually eight. So what gives?"

"Oh, didn't you buy the dog guardian story?"

Madison's lips turned at the corners and her eyes narrowed. Maxwell laughed out loud, his baritone voice booming above the common park noises. "All right, well, I happen to have as two of my nearest and dearest friends a St. Bernard named Mr. Bigs and a rottweiler named Boss. I've been a dog lover since I was a kid. Dogs are everything that people have a hard time being—loyal, compassionate and predictable," Maxwell said.

"Well, I can't argue with that," Madison said wistfully.

"So is it just you and Brandy? Two beautiful females all on your own?"

Madison appreciated his tactful and charming way of attempting to find out if she was single. She was pleased that, despite how charming and attractive Maxwell was, she was *not* single, but deeply in love with the only man for whom she had eyes.

A smile spread across Madison's face.

"Brandy doesn't actually belong to me. I've just been her walker for a few months. I've never had a dog of my own," she said.

"Really? Not even as a kid?"

"Nope. My mother wasn't an animal lover and the last thing she would allow was one running around, scratching up her hardwood floors."

"Do you still live at home?" Maxwell asked.

"Nope. I relocated to New York from North Carolina about eighteen months ago."

"You're from the N.C.? Get outta here. I was born in Virginia in Danville, right on the border of Caswell County, North Carolina."

"Okay, a country boy?" Madison smiled.

"Yep…transplanted like you, I guess. I've been up north for the past seven years since I did my undergraduate studies at Columbia University. Much as I like New York, part of me still misses the relaxed pace of home. Guess I'm still a Southern boy at heart. How about you?"

"Well, I have to say that I absolutely love it up here. It's been an eye-opener, to say the least, but I'm feeling more like a native New Yorker every day."

By the time they reached the station, Maxwell was certain that he wanted to get to know the petite beauty a lot better. While Brandy drank two bowls of the fresh water provided by the handlers, Maxwell and Madison chatted. When Brandy had had her fill of water and was back on her feet, bouncing around, Madison prepared to head home.

"Well, Maxwell, it was a pleasure meeting you and thank you for rescuing Brandy here from dehydration. I was so wrapped up in my thoughts that I didn't realize how much I'd walked her. I guess she's not as spry as she used to be."

"I don't think any of us are," Maxwell said, giving Brandy a playful tap on the back. "Listen, Madison, how'd you like to get together sometime…for drinks or dinner? I mean, I'm not sure if you're involved or anything, so please, let me know if I'm overstepping," Maxwell said.

"Maxwell, I'm flattered. However, I'm in a relationship," Madison said.

"Ouch. All right then, I guess that's that. Perhaps I'll see you again on the dog walk?" he asked.

"Perhaps."

Madison tightened her grip on Brandy's leash and headed out of the park. If she hadn't known what to do when she first arrived in the park that evening, she knew now. She would lay it all on the line and let Steve know that she was willing to relocate to accommodate his life or make room for him here in hers. The bottom line was that she loved him and she wanted to be with him. It was time that they figured out how to make it work because the only person she wanted to stroll through the park with was her man, Stevenson Elliott.

## Chapter 19

The rain came down in droves, pelting the ragtop of her mother's yellow Mustang convertible as Madison maneuvered cautiously down the slick streets of downtown Charlotte. Madison had become a more conscious and considerate driver ever since Kennedy's car accident. There was a time when she'd cut people off in a heartbeat, always in a rush even if she was only going to the supermarket. Madison had been like many drivers—impatient and critical of her fellow motorists. However, it took nearly losing her only sibling to make her realize that there was never a good enough reason to tempt fate, especially when Mother Nature was unleashing her fury like she was today.

Madison glanced at the console of the car, reading the blue illuminated digital clock. It was eleven-fifteen in the morning and she had eight hours until Steve's arrival.

A month had passed since her return from England and she could not believe how much she missed him. When he'd told her that the Wesco transition had finally been closed and settled, freeing him up considerably, she'd invited him to North Carolina to spend a few days with her family. A cousin of hers was getting married and Madison wanted him there to meet Kennedy, her husband Malik, and the rest of the Daniels clan. Madison had also cryptically informed him that there were things that she wanted to talk to him about and they could only be done in person. She assured him that it was all good and that was enough for him.

In actuality, Steve was honored by her request to share the festivities with her and he booked a flight without wasting any time. He did not dare tell Madison that he'd told his parents he was going skiing in Switzerland with Neil and some other friends of theirs. Despite her earlier declarations, he did exactly what she'd resisted and let sleeping dogs lie. Not talking about Steve's parents or the tabloids did not make their concerns disappear, but it did make it less intrusive on their relationship, freeing them up to just concentrate on each other.

Joseph and Elmira Daniels could not have been happier when they learned that Steve was coming for a visit. It was obvious that not only did they approve of their daughter's new beau, but they were also anxiously awaiting the news that he would soon be elevated from boyfriend status to the position of husband. After years of worrying and praying over Madison, watching her rowdy behavior lead her from one scandal into the next, they were comforted to know that she had found someone who was not only from the right background and breeding, but was also a hardworking grounded young man.

When Steve arrived, it was as if the time they'd spent apart had never happened. She melted in his arms and they greeted each other with the enthusiasm and familiarity of a couple who'd been together for decades.

Over a backyard barbecue, with Malik and Steve manning the grill, the family got a chance to know the young man who had captured Madison's heart just when they'd all believed she'd never settle down.

"Girl, he's fine. The next time you take a trip overseas, please put me in your suitcase and take me with you so I can find me some cute foreigner, too," cousin Erica exclaimed. "Ooh, I just love his accent. It's sexy."

"All right, ladies, stop drooling over my sister's man. He's taken." Kennedy smiled.

Later, when the sisters were alone, it was Kennedy's turn to drool. "You done good, little sister. He's a very nice guy. Funny, intelligent…he and Dad seem to be hitting it off well. Hmph, at least you don't have to worry about Mommy turning her nose up at him, especially given the fact that he comes with a whole bunch of zeros after his last name."

"Stop it, Kennedy. I told you before, he doesn't even consider himself as being rich," Madison said.

"Yeah, I know what you said, but I will tell you this— Mommy may have accepted Malik, finally, but if Steve came in here, as brown as he is and broke on top of that… Well, let's just say I don't think she would have been rolling out the red carpet. She's my mother and I love her dearly, but she's as shallow as a baking pan."

Cousin Vicky's wedding was a splendid affair, at which the who's who of the South were all in attendance. Steve met so many cousins, uncles, aunts and dear family friends that after a while he stopped trying to keep names and faces straight in his head. Growing up as an only child, in a household that consisted of him, his parents and the various domestic help that came and went over the years, he had no frame of reference for what he experienced at that wedding and the days surrounding it. It was heart-warming and slightly unnerving at the same time.

The small manila envelope fell to the floor as Steve reached past it in order to pick up the car keys from Madison's dressing table. He'd needed to get the shaving cream and other toiletries he'd purchased the day before out of the trunk of the car. Madison had gone jogging with her sister and he'd slept in, trying to shake off the residue of the tequila shots he'd had competing against Malik the night before.

After the wedding reception, Steve, Madison, Malik and Kennedy went out for a night on the town, which included nachos and black-bean dip, hours of salsa dancing at a downtown club and a whole lot of drinking. They had a great time together, proving that despite the differences in their socioeconomic and cultural backgrounds, four people could hit it off and enjoy themselves as if they were old friends.

In the morning, Steve was paying for that good time with a headache that made him clumsy and sluggish. He stooped to pick the envelope up from the floor, noticing the edge of a colored photograph sticking out as he did so. Cu-

riosity got the better of him, and he stuck his hand inside
and retrieved two dozen glossy, colored photos. What he
saw caused him to sink to the bed, his legs feeling weak
beneath him.

Photograph after photograph of Madison and a guy with
the backdrop of a lake, mountains and scenic forest were
displayed before his eyes. Sometimes they were joined by
another couple and there were a few photographs of
Madison alone. He turned the envelope over to the front
and read the return address to learn that they had come
from a Liza Penning from New York. Steve realized that
Liza was Madison's childhood friend whom he had yet to
meet. Slowly, he put two and two together and recalled the
camping trip Madison had gone on with Liza a few months
back. She had told him all about it, or so he'd thought. She
and Liza had spent the weekend roasting marshmallows
and painting their nails. At no point did she mention that
there had been more entertainment on the program besides
night crickets and hooting owls.

Steve shoved the pictures back into the envelope, tossing
them angrily onto the dressing table where he'd found
them. He paced the floor, trying to will the sting of jealousy
to stay at bay, but fought a losing battle. Once again he was
being hammered over the head with the fact that Madison
was an attractive woman to whom men were drawn like
ants marching to a picnic. He didn't hate the fact that she
was a sexy, alluring woman. What bothered him was that
no matter where she was or what she was doing, she
seemed to have a hard time refusing the attention of a man.
He asked himself if he could ever truly trust in the belief
that he was the man, the one and only man for her, when

every time he turned around there were innuendos and suggestions to the contrary.

By the time Madison and Kennedy returned to the house, Steve had lost his battle to quell his anguish. She entered the bedroom, expecting to find a still sleeping Steve, since the breakfast she'd set aside for him remained untouched in the kitchen.

"Hey, sleepyhead, you are awake. How are you feeling now?" she asked.

Steve's expression stopped her in her tracks.

"What happened?" she asked, immediately aware from the strained look on his unshaven face that something was troubling him.

Without answering, Steve walked over to the dressing table and picked up the envelope. He moved closer to Madison, opened the envelope, and when he was within a couple of feet of her, he held it up and poured the contents out. The photographs landed on the plush carpet at her feet, some of them faceup and others facedown.

"What the hell is this?" he asked.

Madison picked up a few of the pictures, and sifted through them before returning her gaze to Steve's face.

"Calm down, please," she said evenly.

Steve checked his tone, reminding himself that he was in Madison's parents' home. He walked over to the bedroom door and closed it softly.

"What is this?" he repeated when he had returned to the spot where Madison remained standing.

"These are photographs that Liza took while we were camping. If you're asking who the guys are, they're two brothers who were staying in a cabin nearby. We spent an afternoon with them canoeing and sightseeing," Madison said.

She tossed the photos on the dressing table and sat down on the edge of the queen-sized brass bed. There was a heavy silence in the room.

"And?" Steve asked as if there had never been a pause in the conversation.

"And what? There is no *and*. We met some people, hung out a little bit and came home. End of story."

"If it was so simple, why didn't you mention any of this when you told me about the trip?"

"Steve, let me tell you something. I don't do suspicion, okay? I don't do paranoia or accusation. Those are things that I just don't do. So I'm not going to sit here and answer twenty questions. I've told you that it was nothing and you're going to need to take my word for it because I'm done."

"I can't believe you're catching an attitude with me. What if the tables were turned? Would you be so understanding?"

Madison rose and walked over to Steve. She stood in front of him, less than a few inches separating them. Slowly, she reached up and touched the side of his face, her eyes trained on his.

"I trust you, Steve. It's just as simple as that. I trust you with my love and my heart. Do you trust me?"

Madison raised her other hand, placing it on the other side of Steve's face. Her touch still electrified him, rendering him incapable of feeling anything but love for her. Her eyes told him what he needed to hear. He wished that every time he felt fear or envy, he could simply look into her eyes and have his soul washed within the security of her love.

By the time Steve left North Carolina, the lovers' little

spat had all but been forgotten. The timing did not seem right to bring up the subject of moving toward a more permanent phase in their relationship as Madison had planned on doing, but she hoped that it would soon get there. In the meantime, they parted feeling cautiously optimistic, wondering if strife at this early stage in their relationship was indicative of what was to come.

# Chapter 20

Steve kicked the large brown box in front of him, wincing at the immediate pain that shot up his foot. He cursed as he shoved the box aside, his annoyance almost entirely directed at himself. When he'd come up with the idea that led him into the records department of Elliott Corporation, it had seemed like a great one. Now, as he looked around the room he was in, a two-hundred-square-foot area at the back of the company's main file room, he realized that he'd taken on a tedious and extensive task.

The twentieth anniversary of the launching of Elliott Corporation was approaching. In an effort to smooth the stormy waters with his father, Steve wanted to do something special for him. It was during his long flight home from North Carolina that he had come up with the idea and he was eager to implement it as soon as he arrived. He had decided to create a replica of the original Elliott Corporation headquarters and plant, which had been subjected to a complete overhaul and redesign in the early nineties. His plan was to have the model built and presented to his father to display in the current lobby of the corporate offices. In addition to original blueprints, he was looking for photographs and other design plans for the building.

Steve knew that his father would love the model but, more importantly, he hoped that it would help them begin a dialogue that they both were too stubborn and proud to initiate. Gregory wanted him to just acquiesce to his demands and forget, as if the past few months had not happened. For his part, Steve wanted his father to acknowledge that strong-arming him into submission was wrong. He hoped Gregory Elliott could open himself up to the possibility of getting to know Madison. This last wish was a fantasy that Steve feared he would have to let go of. However, he decided that his efforts would be well worth it if they at least opened the doors.

After a couple of hours of searching, he found most of what he had been looking for. He also found records and journals in his father's handwriting that showed the initial planning for the corporation and documentation of the progress over the first ten years. For his entire life he had heard the stories from other people, including his mother, of his father's dogged determination and diligence in making his dream come true. Seeing the stages of the actual planning and development of that dream in black and white made an even greater impression on Steve. He read through the journals and other paperwork in awe at how his father had been able to take nothing and turn it into something single-handedly. As the night wore on, Steve decided to pack up a couple of small boxes that he hadn't yet been able to go through in the hopes that over the next few days he could pore over them leisurely. Perhaps as he read more about how his father was able to build an amazing career for himself, it would help him in his own quest to find his life's passion.

Janice turned to face her husband and a shiver passed immediately up and down her spine when she regarded him. He was extremely serious about what he'd just said to her and for a moment she was reminded of that man she'd married three decades ago back in Jamaica who had been hell-bent on getting out of the impoverished country no matter what he had to do.

"Honey, I know you are upset, but really, isn't this a bit extreme?" she asked, her voice cool.

"Janice, I would expect you to say that. You've done nothing but coddle and indulge that boy since the day he was born. But no more. It stops here. He cannot just run around doing whatever he wants to do without consequences. I have worked too hard to build this company and to provide for this family. I will not have him jeopardize that just because he thinks he's in love."

"But, Gregory—"

"This is not open for discussion, Janice. Since he met that woman he has lied to us, purposely misled us and carried out various acts of omission. Not to mention his irresponsibility in carrying out his duties at the Elliott Corporation. He's been missing in action for the past week, going off with no regard to his obligations to the company.

We find out that instead of being in Switzerland with his friends, he's off at that…that tramp's house."

Gregory fumed as he said this. He was incensed by the fact that his son would disobey him and disregard his wishes the way he had. Janice quietly studied her husband, stunned by the intensity of his anger but not entirely surprised. In recent years, Gregory had seemed as though he was mellowing out. She was well aware of how severe he could be, especially when it came to his expectations not being met. Yet tonight, he reminded her of a younger, more ambitious man who still had so much to prove and so much to accomplish. She'd always wished that he had been more of an expressive father toward his son. He was not the type of dad who ever threw the ball around with his son on the weekends or helped him build a model airplane. Gregory ran a tight ship, both at home and at the office. He did nothing with Stevenson that was not designed to provide a lesson.

As a result, Stevenson had grown up being very respectful and full of direction, yet she'd often wished she could have seen her child smile more, laugh just a little bit louder and have fun with his father. She had tried to give Steve all of the nurturing and love that his father failed to show. In good or bad times, it was she who provided the hugs and the kisses, where Gregory provided the discipline and scolding. Now that Stevenson was a grown man, it was still her hope that father and son would find a way to come together and to bond in the way that some men did, either at a football game or out on the lake fishing or something of that nature. It hadn't happened yet and that was one of the greatest disappointments of her life. It seemed that instead of growing softer, Gregory was growing harder and this latest position he was taking was a sign that he was not about to change.

"Gregory, I'm sure you know what's best. I just wish that there was another way for you to get Stevenson to understand your point of view. Are you sure this is the right way to approach him?" she asked, her voice soft and soothing.

"Yes, I'm sure," Gregory said.

He placed the document he'd shown her in the top drawer of his desk, an indication that as far as he was concerned, the conversation was over. Janice walked out of the study, heading for the master bedroom, her steps as heavy as her heart. Even while she continued to hope for the best, she knew instinctively that things were headed for the worst.

## Chapter 21

Steve looked from one of his parents to the other. He then looked at the copy of his employment contract that lay on the breakfast table between them. He'd returned to England the night before and once again had been summoned out to his parents' house.

"What are you saying, Dad?" he asked incredulously, certain that he had not heard his father correctly.

"What I'm saying, son…what *we* are saying is that you have a responsibility to this family and an obligation to the legacy I've built for us. If we cannot trust your judgment in your personal life, there is no way that we can trust you to make sound decisions for the company."

"What a crock of shit! You cannot be serious with this."

"Stevenson, you watch your tongue, young man," Janice gasped.

"No, Mother, I will not watch my tongue. It seems to me that that's precisely what I've been doing all this time and where has it gotten me?"

Gregory slammed his fist onto the blown glass table emphatically, his jaw muscle trembling with poorly suppressed rage. "Stevenson, you have behaved recklessly and without a thought to this family's name and reputation. You will either abide by our regulations or you will find yourself out on your own. If you sincerely think that you know best in these affairs, then perhaps you do not belong at the Elliott Corporation. Maybe it is time for you to move on."

Steve looked at his father, suddenly feeling an emotion that was close to hatred boiling within him. "Move on? To what should I move on? You know as well as I do that everything I've done for the past ten years of my life has revolved around the company. From my education to all of my work experience— I have worked damned hard for you and for the company. I deserve my place there and how dare you suggest otherwise!"

It was Steve's turn to seethe as he jumped up from the table. The chair in which he had been sitting tipped backward at his sudden movement, crashing loudly to the floor. He moved away from the table, preferring to put some distance between himself and his parents for the moment. He leaned on the black wrought-iron rail of the balcony. They were on the south side of the house and from this vantage point there was a view of the lake that ran along the length of the house, eventually feeding into the river Mersey about six miles farther south. Steve stared out at the water, wishing that he were anywhere but there right now. He closed his eyes, trying to capture a glimpse of

Madison's smile or anything that could distract him from the incredible clash of wills that was brewing on his parents' balcony that morning.

"Stevenson, we sincerely do not like that things have come to this, but we also feel as though you've left us no alternative."

This was his mother speaking. Her voice was soft and soothing, as though she was offering him a spoonful of honey and rum like she did when he was a little boy and suffering from the sore throats that had plagued him persistently. Steve turned to face her, leaning his back against the railing. Her words belied the expression on her face but he knew that even if she disagreed with the demands his father was making, she was not in a position to do anything to assist him. His father had always made it clear that while Janice was in charge of matters on the home front, the business aspects of their life were none of her concern. And she had always stood by her husband, wrong or right.

"Dad, are you telling me that if I don't agree to break off my relationship with Madison, you are not going to renew my employment contract?"

"Yes, Stevenson. That is precisely what I'm telling you. Your contract expires at the end of the month, so I'd suggest you make a decision posthaste," Gregory replied, his face stoic and his voice cold.

"And what about the board of directors? Are they co-signing this blackmail or haven't you run it by them?" Steve asked, disbelief that his father had gone to these lengths still registering in his voice.

"I am Elliott Corporation. Me. One day, I hope that that title will be passed on to you, but I can assure you that if

I can't trust your judgment, I certainly won't hand my life's work over to you."

Steve heard nothing else that his parents had to say to him that afternoon, nor anything he said in return. His mind grew numb to their words and his, as he tried to find the courage within himself to tell his father what he could do with his job. On principle alone, he wanted to stand there and tear up the employment contract that was being used to make him dance like a puppet, and drop it on the floor at his father's feet. However, that moment never came, and the realization that he could not make himself do that dealt him a vicious blow. He stumbled from his parents' home and drove aimlessly until the gas meter of his car indicated that he was nearly out of fuel. He filled up at the nearest station and returned to his apartment in Manchester. By the time he'd arrived back at home, he was no closer to seeing a resolution to his problems. He felt an instinctive urge to call Madison, having grown so used to her soothing voice and ability to relax him with a word or simply her laugh. However, if he called her, he would have to tell her that she—or more precisely, their relationship— was the source of his troubles and to do that to her would be cruel. Instead, he suffered in silence.

# Chapter 22

Steve's misery intensified as the days progressed. He spent his days working numbly, his mind barely able to stay focused on any particular task for more than a few minutes at a time, but knowing that if he didn't keep busy, he would lose it. At night he took long walks, trying to think and to clear his head of all of the conflicting emotions with which he struggled. While it pained him to do so, he took to avoiding Madison's phone calls or cutting their conversations short, under the guise of being extremely busy at work. Every time he did so, he felt a tremendous surge of guilt, his conscience gnawing at him. Conflicted between his feelings for her and the pressure being placed on him by his parents, Steve grappled for the clarity that would enable him to make the right decision.

"Hello, Steve, this is your mother. I called you at the

office, but Sherri told me that you were working from home today. I was hoping you'd come out to the house and have dinner with me. Your father expects to be out late and, well, you know how I hate to eat alone. Please call me as soon as you get this message…or just pop over."

Steve was lying across his bed when his mother left her message on his answering machine. He made no move to pick up the call, preferring to just let her talk to the tape. He knew that she meant well, but he was not in the mood to talk to her. In fact, he wasn't in the mood to talk to anyone, which is precisely why he'd stayed home today, alone in his apartment. When his cell phone rang for the fourth time that day, he glanced at it. It was Madison calling. She'd called him the night before and he'd feigned fatigue, promising to call her back in the morning, which he didn't do. They'd barely spoken in the days since his quarrel with his parents because he simply did not trust himself to talk to her and not break down.

Steve flipped the phone open, putting it to his ear. "Hello."

"Hey you, are you busy?" Madison asked.

Steve's heart lurched at the sound of her cheerful voice. Again, he was pressed by the urge to just say to hell with his father and run as fast as he could toward Madison.

"A little bit. What's up?" he said, attempting to keep his voice cool.

"Not much. I volunteered this morning at an animal shelter downtown. Oh, Steve, it was so much fun. I mean, it's hard looking at some of those animals—the ones who've been abused or abandoned, but I'll tell you, they are so forgiving. There was this little rabbit that someone had dropped off and he acted just like a baby or something.

When I picked him up, he wiggled his nose and just let me hold him in my arms. Oh, I had a blast."

"Sounds like it. Boy, I wonder why you don't get all giddy when talking about me, too," Steve teased.

"Nah, you're not as cute as a fuzzy little rabbit," Madison joked.

Steve laughed, a tight, unenthusiastic sound spilling from his vocal cords.

"Listen, babe, I've got to run. I've got a lot going on today," he lied.

Madison said she understood and hung up after sending a kiss through the phone. And so their conversations went until after a week of short or nonexistent telephone calls, Madison grew suspicious and confronted him.

"What's going on with you, Steve?"

"Nothing," he said, knowing full well that his erratic and distant behavior was wearing thin with her.

"Steve, come on. Talk to me," Madison pleaded, beginning to feel like a broken record.

She was growing tired of the ups and downs of the relationship, but at the same time, was willing to do whatever it took to make sure that they not merely survived as a couple, but flourished. The first step, she believed, was open communication.

"Did I do something? Say something, Steve. You've been…I don't know, different lately."

Steve sighed, running his hand across his head. It was late and he'd just come in from the office after his father had dumped a load of reports on his desk, which he claimed needed to be analyzed and summarized by the next day. He'd glared at his father behind his back, but held his tongue as he accepted the papers and watched the elder Elliott retreat. They'd barely exchanged words in the past couple of weeks, and it appeared that Gregory was growing increasingly uncomfortable. Just the day before, when Steve had passed him and a small group of executives at the elevator bank, Gregory had invited him to join them for lunch and seemed crushed when Steve had declined.

Something had to give, that much was obvious to Steve. He could not go on distancing himself from everyone and brooding over the situation. He also knew that Madison was the last person who deserved the brunt of his sour mood.

"Madison, there's nothing wrong. I've just been working hard. Look, you said you understood and respected the fact that I have a demanding job. We're not high-school sweethearts, Madison. I can't ditch football practice and meet you by the bleachers, okay?"

"Whoa…where the heck did that come from? Steve, I'm not making demands on you or your time, so if that's the impression you got, you can just put that right out of your mind. You know what? Forget it. Why don't you give me a call when you have the time? Or better yet, why don't you have your secretary pencil me in and let me know when it's a good time to call you back?" Madison snapped.

She'd had about all that she could stand of his icy abruptness and infrequent conversations. She didn't know what was going on, but she certainly knew that things had taken that turn in the road that she had been afraid might happen. She knew that the long-distance relationship was getting to her, and assumed that it was getting to him as well. All he needed to do was to say the words, and she would be there, of that she was certain. She had already weighed all the pros and cons and decided that she would move to be with her man if he asked. But he didn't.

"I'll talk to you later," was all he said before hanging up the telephone.

It was two days before he called her again. Two days in which she, at first, sulked and worried. Eventually, her concerns morphed into anger and frustration at the way he seemed to be deliberately pushing her away. When he called, first her apartment phone and then her cellular, she didn't answer. Her stubborn pride, always having been the source of her most destructive behavior, refused to allow her to appear as if she had been waiting by the phone for him to get around to calling her. Instead she didn't answer, but then played back his messages right after he'd left them. His voice sounded almost like normal, although beneath the surface she heard a quiet agitation that even his apologetic words and sweet terms of endearment could not mask.

Madison asked herself why she did not pick up the phone and call him back at that moment. Looking back at a later time, she realized that perhaps fear had prevented her from doing so. When Steve called her again later that night, and their hesitant conversation turned into a shouting match, she understood better why she had not picked up his initial calls. Innately, she had known that the promise of happy days, as fragrant as fields of flowers, was about to be snatched from beneath her and it was due to an instinct of self-preservation that she attempted to avoid that cruel twist of fate. Regrettably, she had to face the fact that all avoidance did was offer false hope while it delayed the inevitable.

# Chapter 23

In the end it was a defeated Steve who simply gave up. He reconciled that there would be no way that he and Madison could be happy with the amount of pressure his parents were placing on them. When it was just a matter of the annoyance brought on by the gossip magazine reporters who had seemed to launch a campaign on Madison, staking her out everywhere she went, he thought that he could handle it. Every time he saw her name or face splashed across the pages of one of those rags, he told himself that it would die down and their relationship would eventually become old news.

But added to that problem, which was like having a splinter in your finger and being unable to eject it, was the reminder of the photographs of her and her camping friends. He still felt a pang of jealousy when he recalled the glossy images of her smiling in the company of another man. He'd accepted her explanation and assertion that it was innocent, but it stayed with him like a sore. In his heart of hearts he asked himself over and over again if he could truly trust her to be true to him, yet with the weight that that organ was carrying, it was no wonder that he could not get it to provide an answer.

The cherry on top of this melted sundae was his parents. It would be a brand-new ice age before he got them to warm up to Madison, of this he was certain. Even without his father's ultimatum, Steve reasoned that their disapproving attitude and behavior would do nothing but trigger Madison's scorn for them. He went a step further, envisioning that their lives together would be spent between feuding families, quite like Shakespeare's Capulets and Montagues, as her parents fought to defend her honor. He felt weary in his bones, not strong enough to take one minute more.

Yet had Steve been true to himself, he would have acknowledged that the idea of being tossed out into the world on his own, without the stability of his father's business, money and prestige, scared him. He had never held another job; had never even gone on an interview. For a long time he had considered taking some other avenue or path of his own choosing, but now that the prospect was real, he comprehended the reality that he had no other training. He had acquired nothing of his own. The idea of striking out, as a black man, without so much as a letter of recommendation, petrified him. He crumbled beneath the pressure and shamefully took a road that was less than honorable.

"Madison, I don't quite know how to say this, so I guess I'll just say it. Meeting you was one of the highlights of my entire life. If things were different…well, I know that they're not, but I just wish they were," Steve rambled.

He drank two shots of tequila before picking up the telephone and one more as he waited for Madison to pick up the line. It was six o'clock in the morning, her time, and when the phone rang, the alarm in Madison's voice almost deterred him from his planned course of action. Almost.

"Steve, what are you trying to say to me?" Madison asked, gripping the phone so tightly that the skin around her knuckles stretched and lightened.

He smacked his hand against his forehead, wishing that he could make his brain get the words to come out of his mouth with some semblance of logic. Yet he also realized that there was no logic to what he was doing and that despite how illogical it felt to his heart, he felt that he had no choice.

"I just think that we got a little too serious too quickly. I think maybe we should slow things down a little bit," Steve said, thrusting the words out of his mouth forcefully, making them sound a little more harsh than he'd intended.

"Wasn't it you who said that there was no such place as too fast?" Madison asked.

"I wasn't thinking clearly, Madison. I met you and I kinda lost my head for a minute."

"And so now you've found it?"

"I guess you could say that. Look, I just think that we should maybe explore other options."

"Other options. Steve, are you saying that you're seeing someone else?"

"No, that's not what I'm saying. I mean, I think we both should—should see other people, that is. And as for the trip…we should cancel that trip to Italy. At least until we've worked through things. I just feel like we've rushed things a bit and, well, we should just slow down a little," Steve said.

Madison sat in stunned silence after hanging up the telephone. Their plans for a romantic getaway to Italy had sustained her while they were apart, as she had been looking forward to spending time away from everyone with Steve and thought he had felt the same way. She did not quite know what to make of Steve's request, but realized that the signs had been present for the past few weeks. Had she bothered to look at them, she would have seen that they'd been headed in that direction for quite a while. What had started out as a fiery love affair had seemingly fizzled and been reduced to a low simmer. Though her feelings for Steve had not diminished, she, too, had begun to wonder if it was too much to expect for them to ride off into the sunset. Instead of giving in to the sadness and disappointment that threatened to take her over, she reasoned that perhaps Steve was right. Taking a step back from the relationship for a while would help them to determine if their love was indeed strong enough to endure.

It was with a loose grip on a thread of optimism that Madison said goodbye to Steve. He promised to call her at the end of the week and she accepted that promise with the same amount of optimism with which it was given.

## Chapter 24

"I'm glad you called, Steve. This was nice," Genevieve said as she and Steve strolled past a row of beautiful Georgian houses.

Steve tucked the edge of Genevieve's Hermès scarf, which had been flapping in the wind, into the collar of her coat.

"Yes, I had a good time tonight," Steve answered genuinely.

It had been weeks since he'd smiled, much less laughed. Spending the evening with Genevieve had been a good cure for what ailed him. His mother had pushed him to call her, and finally, when he felt as if he would go crazy if he spent one minute more alone at his home, he did.

They'd had dinner at a Mediterranean-style restaurant—the first full-course meal that he could recall digesting in weeks. Afterward, they'd sat in for a set at Andral's, a trendy nightspot where Neil's youngest brother played bass in the band. The evening had unfolded at an easy pace in which Steve did much of the talking, prompted by the occasional well-placed question from Genevieve. They talked about politics and various socioeconomic crises that persisted around the world. It was heavy conversation for a first date, but Steve was pleased to learn that Genevieve was quite the activist. She shared with him the news that she sat on the People's Initiative Board for African Reform. Her purpose was in helping to eradicate the HIV and AIDS crisis that was plaguing the poor in various African nations through fund-raising and increasing public information and awareness. He was impressed more than anything else by the passion with which she spoke about her various activities.

"What is it like being the daughter of a government minister?"

"What's it like? I don't know…I suppose my dad is the same as any other dad. His job is his job, and he's tough and imposing, but at home, he's just Dad."

"It must be difficult having government agents lurking about all the time, watching your father's back. That would drive me crazy."

"No, I never really felt like they were in the way. Maybe when we went on family holiday or something, but otherwise, it was really no big deal. What about you? Your dad is *the* Gregory Elliott, Mr. Billion-Dollar Man himself. What's it like growing up loaded?" Genevieve laughed.

"I always tell people the same thing when they ask that— my father is wealthy, but I'm not," Steve said lightheartedly.

Genevieve was tactful in her approach as she touched

on the subject of Steve's recent publicity. In turn, he was extremely candid with her about Madison.

"Madison Daniels is a lovely woman. I'm very proud to have met her," he said sincerely.

"I'm sorry that things didn't work out between the two of you," Genevieve offered.

She did not think it appropriate to let on that she and his mother had had extensive conversations about Madison and the fact that the Elliotts did not approve of her. While Genevieve herself thought that the woman was attractive, she agreed that she was common. Coming from a prestigious family like the Elliotts, Steve needed a woman of a certain breeding and reputation, attributes that Madison appeared to be sorely lacking.

"Well, these things happen. What's that old expression? 'It's better to have loved and lost than never to have loved at all.' I don't think truer words have ever been spoken."

"Spoken like a true romantic. So, Mr. Elliott, are you truly the dreamy idealist that you paint yourself to be?"

"Ha! Now, that's a good one. A dreamy idealist? Let me think a little over that one. I believe in love, although I haven't had much experience in the matter. I don't believe that love conquers all, which I guess makes me a little jaded. But overall, I'd have to say that I am an optimist disguised as a realist who is an undercover optimist. How's that for self-analysis?" Steve laughed.

"Pretty good. Do you know how much that would have cost you had a shrink diagnosed you?"

"What about you, Ms. Daltrey? You've let me run on and on at the mouth all evening and you've failed to tell me much about you, other than the fact that you want to save the world and you're allergic to cats."

"There's really not much else to tell. I'm a daddy's girl through and through. My mother might tell you I was a bit spoiled as a child, but I'd deny it. I love to travel, I'm a vegan and, perhaps the most telling thing would be the fact that I am a hopeless romantic. Fairy tales are the best love stories to me because they always end with happily ever after."

The date was a beginning and while Steve attempted to throw himself into it, he realized that he was still stuck on another ending. It was this thought of finding a fresh start once the happily ever after did not happen that brought to mind other thoughts that Steve had believed he'd tucked away for good. One night, after working late with his father on some notes for a presentation he was preparing for a meeting with a government agency, he worked up the nerve to verbalize questions he'd had for a long time.

"Dad, can I ask you something?" Steve said as they packed up for the night.

"Of course," Gregory responded.

Gregory was not a man who showed his emotions, unless that emotion was related to anger. He could not bring himself to express his sincere joy at the fact that he and Steve had managed to get back on speaking terms, but he jumped on any chance he could to spend time with and talk to Steve.

"When was the last time you spoke to anyone from back home?" Steve asked.

"Back home?" Gregory asked, genuinely confused since, for him, right where they were in England was and always had been home.

"Back in Jamaica. When is the last time you've had contact with any of the family in Jamaica?" Steve asked.

"Where is this coming from?" Gregory asked.

He was stunned by his son's line of questioning, having thought the inquisitive child had long ago given way to the man.

"It's not coming from anywhere. It's just something I've been curious about."

"Stevenson, I haven't spoken to anyone back there in years. You and your mother are my family. It's as simple as that," Gregory said, his tone indicative of the desire to put an end to the conversation.

Steve held his tongue, understanding that as usual, his father had no intentions of delving into a life that for him was long ago put to death and buried.

# Chapter 25

Gazing off the starboard side of the yacht out into the blackness of the open waters, Steve tried to shake off the melancholy mood that he felt descending upon him. His heart matched the blue-black of the night and even the most brilliant stars in the sky could not spark a light within him.

"A penny for your thoughts?" Genevieve asked, appearing at his side.

Steve turned to face her, startled at her classic beauty once again. "That's a very Yankee expression. I thought you despised all things American?"

Genevieve had made that revelation when Steve lapsed into an extended description of the eclectic mixture of people, sights, sounds and smells that could be found on any street in New York's Manhattan. She'd listened with detached interest before informing him that of all the places of interest in the world to visit, the United States was just about last on her list.

"No, not all things. I hear they make the best cheese steak sandwiches," Genevieve laughed.

Steve halfheartedly joined in on her laughter.

"What's the matter?" she asked again, placing her long, delicate fingers on his forearm.

Steve ignored the fact that her touch did nothing for him.

"Are you thinking of her again?"

Genevieve was nothing if not blunt. Steve shook his head in denial.

"No, no, I wasn't," he lied.

Genevieve was not fooled, but appreciated his attempt at sparing her feelings. She'd known what she was up against early on, but that did not deter her. Her parents were right—Steve was a very good catch and she had every intention of catching him.

All of her life Genevieve Daltrey had been groomed to marry well. She'd finished charm school with flying colors, taken years of ballet and performance arts, had become fluent in three languages and was accomplished at both the violin and the harpsichord. She was everything a rich and powerful executive could want and need in a wife, and on top of all that, she was beautiful. With the help of two years of braces, forced dieting and minor corrective surgery on her nose, Genevieve had been transformed from an awkward duckling to emerge from her teenage years as a lovely swan. Here she was at twenty-six years old, poised and graceful and ready to fulfill her dreams. All she had to do was to get the man of her dreams to understand how perfect she was for him.

Genevieve reached up to touch the side of Steve's face, running two soft fingers up and down the fuzzy hair that grew along his jawline. He clasped her fingers in his hand, leaned forward and brushed his lips against hers. Her mouth gave in to his as he kissed her softly. They parted and he placed his arm around her shoulder, pulling her against him. They stared in silence out into the night, their thoughts as divided as two people's could be.

Not much time passed before Genevieve and Steve became an official couple. The reports of sightings of the pair had begun to make the news and although Steve allowed himself to get swept up in the current of a romantic fairy tale, he could not make himself feel much like the dashing prince who woos his fair maiden. It was easier to just go with the flow of things, and spending time with Genevieve provided a distraction from less productive thoughts. He hoped that the more time he shared with Genevieve, the closer he would grow toward her emotionally, but that did not happen. Instead, all he felt was a sinking sensation in the pit of his stomach as he realized that he was rapidly running out of time. He knew that it would not be long before Madison got wind of his relationship with Genevieve, yet he couldn't find sufficient words or the courage to tell her himself.

The other thing Steve couldn't do was to bring himself to feel toward Genevieve anywhere near the depths of his love for Madison, a fact that his mother advised would change in time.

"Despite what the movies and storybooks try to tell you, enduring love is something that comes with time and commitment," said Janice over dessert one evening when Steve stopped by.

"I don't know if that'll ever happen with Genevieve. I mean, she's wonderful and I've grown to care about her…as a person. I'm just not in love with her," Steve admitted.

"Son, give yourself a chance to love her. Stop holding on to something that is not good for you and make room for Genevieve. I promise you that it will come…in time," Janice said confidently.

Steve tried to block out thoughts of Madison and concentrate on Genevieve. When he kissed her, he would not allow images of Madison to invade his thoughts. Although Genevieve was a beautiful and sexy woman, he could not make himself react to her in more than a physical way. He touched her, enjoying the way her body felt against his, but more out of a human need to be touched than any sort of an emotional attraction. When the question of making love came up, Steve felt an overwhelming sense of relief when Genevieve expressed her desire to remain a virgin until marriage. This gave him a reprieve for the time being, at least until he could separate his feelings and rid himself of memories of Madison's touch that seemed to cling to him.

But everything was going wrong for Steve and he felt powerless to stop it. Especially when one evening after dinner with Genevieve and his parents, his father pulled him into the study for a nightcap and chat. Steve knew that he was in for something unexpected, but he was sorely unprepared for what his father proposed to him that night.

Gregory wasted no time jumping into the real reason he wanted to get Steve alone. Right after he plucked the bottle of brandy from its place inside the wall bar, he began talking. "Son, I know that Genevieve was not your first choice, but she's a lovely woman, wouldn't you agree?"

"Yes, she's great," Steve said.

"She reminds me a lot of your mother, you know. A woman who is not all independent and feisty, but understands that a man needs a mate by his side who will support him and sustain his dreams. I don't think I'd be where I am today without your mother in my corner, cheering me on all the way," he said.

Across his face passed a reflective look that surprised Steve, but it only lasted a second.

"Well, anyway, those are just the thoughts of an old man, I guess. You young guys are too busy looking for rump shakers to think about all of that."

"No, Dad, you're wrong. Most guys my age are looking for a mate who will support them. It's just that we want her to be wrapped up inside a rump shaker," Steve joked.

Gregory laughed with him.

"Dad, I've never heard you talk like this. Is everything all right with you?" Steve asked.

"With me? Oh, yes. Things couldn't be better. Are you aware that the Prime Minister has gotten permission from the Queen to dissolve the current Parliament and has set a date for the general elections?" Gregory said, shifting gears.

"Yes, I've read the elections are to take place by year-end. Why do you bring this up?" Steve asked.

"Well, what you do not know as it is not public knowledge is that Cabinet Member Daltrey, Genevieve's dad, has been slated to take the top spot. Thus, when the current Parliament comes to an end, we probably will be saluting Minister Percy Daltrey as the new head of government."

"Wow, that's a great honor. I'm sure Mr. Daltrey is deserving. I've heard nothing but great things about the man,"

Steve said, still unsure why his father chose this time to have a political conversation.

"Yes, yes. I wholeheartedly agree. Percy and I were talking things over the other day and the change in his position could prove lucrative to both of us. He's always supported the work that we do and, well, securing more government contracts on a regular basis could aid the company's stability from now into the foreseeable future."

"Sounds great," Steve said, not sure of what else his father wanted him to say.

"Yes and Percy and I talked it over," he repeated, pausing to take a swig of his brandy, "and we think that the timing is perfect for you and Genevieve to become engaged."

Steve stiffened, gripping the brandy glass in his hands a bit more tightly.

"Engaged to do what?" he asked.

"Stevenson, your thirtieth birthday is just a couple of years around the corner. It's time you start thinking about your future and settling down. It would make your mother and me rest easier not having to worry about you anymore," Gregory said.

With those words, he pushed Steve back out of the study to rejoin his mother and Genevieve. Once again his father was pulling the strings and Steve was expected to dance.

# Chapter 26

"Ma-Madison, what are you doing here?"

Madison pushed Steve's apartment door open farther, bursting through it without waiting for an invitation.

"I'm here, Steve, like it or not and I want you to tell me to my face that it's over. You tell me that it was all just a lie."

Madison was breathless as she stood in the center of Steve's living room. She saw Genevieve standing there, her mouth agape, without really seeing her. She didn't care about her, nor did she care how she looked or sounded. Water dripped from her locks and ran down her forehead, but she didn't even attempt to wipe it away. Her rain-soaked blouse clung to her breasts. The astonished look on Steve's face was nothing compared to the racing of her heart. Madison had wondered the *why* of it all, from the day that Steve ended their relationship in the cryptic fashion in which he chose to do it. Finally, as she flipped to the society pages of the local newspaper one Sunday morning, she learned the awful truth. Her vision blurred at the words that announced the engagement of Stevenson Elliott and Genevieve Daltrey, England's latest *It* couple. Her humiliation was great, yet her love for Steve remained even greater. Before she could contemplate her actions, she was on a plane with her heart in her hands.

"Genevieve, can you…would you please give us a minute?" Steve asked.

Genevieve opened her mouth to say something, but thought better of it. She turned on her heel and walked away, entering the bedroom and shutting the door behind her.

"Madison, sit down, please," Steve said.

"No, Steve. I'd rather stand, but thank you anyway. Now, would you please just answer my question?"

Her voice was measured and tempered by a strong will to remain calm and collected.

Steve sighed heavily, running his hand across his head roughly. He looked at Madison, then looked away again. He tugged at his beard, his brain a jumble of confused thoughts and conflicting images.

"Steve, I just flew eight hours and halfway across the world. I haven't slept in days. Now that I'm here, I'm tired, wet and I have a pain in my head that feels like I'm being split in two with an axe. At the very least, you can look at me and answer my question," Madison demanded.

She tried her best to sound strong and confident, despite the fact that her insides were shaking like the plane she'd just disembarked had been when it hit that twenty-minute patch of turbulence over the ocean.

"Can I make you a cup of tea?" Steve asked, obviously stalling for time.

The look Madison shot him made him pause as he moved toward the kitchen. He'd run out of time and there was no amount of trickery or skillful dodging that would add another minute to the clock.

"Madison, I'm sorry. I'm so sorry about everything that happened…the way it all turned out. I was not lying to you before…when we met," he said, stumbling over his words.

"You said you loved me," Madison reminded him.

"I did…I wanted to love you, Madison."

"Were you seeing her all along?"

"No! I swear to you, Madison, Genevieve and I had never even met until a couple of months ago," Steve said emphatically.

"Steve, I don't fully understand what's going on here, but I know that I love you. I want to be with you. Now, please tell me I haven't played myself by coming here because I'm willing to risk everything for you. Won't you do the same for me?"

"What do you want from me, Madison? Do you want me to just walk away from my home…denounce my family? Better still, should I run away with you? To where? Where will we go? How will we live? Come on, none of that is realistic, Madison. You've got to see that."

"Why isn't it, Steve? This is not the dark ages. Nobody is going to hunt us down and have us drawn and quartered for loving each other. We can have a life together, Steve, just like we talked about."

"Look, Madison, it just wasn't meant to be. I don't want to stand here and rehash it all. It just wasn't meant to be and it's better that we know now than later. Later…it would have been much harder for both of us."

"What would have been much harder, Steve? Huh? Are you saying that breaking my heart would have been much harder for you? When would it have been harder? When, Steve? After we slept together? After we shared our hopes and dreams with each other? How about after we opened our souls to one another? News flash, Steve—we've been there and done that. It's already too late!" Madison screamed.

"Madison, please—"

"Don't 'Madison, please' me. You tell me right now, Steve, face-to-face, that you love her. You tell me that you feel an ounce for her of what you feel for me."

Madison pointed at the closed bedroom door, her finger a dagger as piercing as her words. She knew that she was yelling, but she didn't care if all of England heard her.

"She's going to be my wife, Madison. Like it or not."

"You didn't answer my question," she challenged.

She had never been less sure of herself, but more sure that she had to put it all on the line. This was too important for her not to.

"Genevieve is going to be my wife. That's all that matters now," Steve said.

Madison stared at him in disbelief. Hot tears formed in her eyes, yet she willed them not to drop. She allowed all the rage she was feeling to bubble to the surface and it spewed from her like hot lava. "You can't answer me, can you?"

She put her hand on his arm and he jumped away from her touch.

"What do you want from me, Madison?" Steve yelled. "I'm so tired of everyone wanting things from me. I can't give you what you want, don't you understand that? Why can't you get that through your head?"

"I hate you, Stevenson Elliott. I hate you," she screamed.

Madison turned toward the door, snatching the knob and trying to open it all in one motion. After two unsuccessful attempts, she managed to get the door open. She charged out into the hallway, picking up speed the farther away from his door that she advanced. Through the blood pounding in her ears she did not hear Steve's rapid footsteps behind her, as he ran after her. Out on the sidewalk he caught up, grabbing her by the shoulder from behind.

"Madison, wait," he begged.

"Get the hell off of me," she screamed in his face.

She smacked at his hands.

"Baby, just listen to me. I never wanted to hurt you. Don't you think it kills me to see what I've done to you. Baby—"

Steve dared to pull Madison into his arms. Too weak and distraught to resist, she gave in to his embrace. And once she was in his arms, leaning against the rock-solid strength of his chest, his racing heart beating against her body, the dam broke and the tears she'd been holding in check began to tumble down her face, soaking his shirt as much as the light rain that was falling.

"Why? Steve, why?"

"Shh, baby, please don't cry. I didn't mean to make you cry," Steve said, his own tears now falling.

He wanted to tell her how tortured he'd been for the past couple of months, knowing that this moment would come and dreading it all the same. He wanted to tell her that he loved her more than life and hurting her was the equivalent of cutting off his own arm. He wanted to kiss her hurt away, love her heartache into oblivion.

"Are you coming home with me?" Madison asked, her voice a cracked whisper.

"Madison…I…I can't. I have a responsibility to my family and the business. I can't just walk away. But, baby, that doesn't mean I have to stop loving you."

"What are you saying to me, Steve?"

"I'm saying that I won't stop loving you. Yes, I have to be here, and yes, my parents are pushing for this wedding to Genevieve. Right now I have to give them what they're asking for, but that doesn't mean it'll be forever."

"So…so you're asking me to wait for you?" Madison asked, staring up at Steve in disbelief. "How long should I wait, Steve? What do you think—a month, a year, ten years or twenty? When will you finally be able to be with me?"

"I don't want to stop being with you, Madison. Maybe…I don't know what I'm saying," Steve said, breaking off.

He looked away, up to the sky and down to the ground, searching for answers that were nowhere to be found.

"I could get to New York a couple of times a year and…and maybe you could fly out here a few times. I could get a small apartment somewhere and we could, we could—"

"We could do what, Steve? Sneak around behind your *wife's* back? You want me to be your secret mistress while you go off and play house with *her?* Oh, my God! Just when I thought this whole thing couldn't get any worse."

"Madison, just think about it…it's all I have to give you right now."

"You know what, Steve? You can just keep that."

Madison turned to walk away, devastation causing her to stagger. Steve reached out, grabbing her forearm to stop her. Madison swung back, her free hand making violent contact with his cheek. He released her, stunned to have been touched by her in a harsh way after growing to live for her caress. Madison didn't waste another minute in making her escape. She ran as fast as her legs could carry her, determined to run all the way back to the United States if she had to.

## Chapter 27

Madison lay on the sofa, her apartment dark and musty from being shut tight for days. She wore nothing but a bathrobe and socks. Half-eaten plates of various foods were strewn across the coffee table in front of her. Save for the shaking of her left foot, it was not immediately apparent whether she was asleep or awake.

The first two days upon her return from Manchester had been hardest. Her stomach had been turned upside down, leaving her without an appetite. After more than forty hours of not eating or drinking anything, she became uncontrollably ill, vomiting brutally every few hours until there was nothing left inside her but air. Now, working on day four of her self-imposed solitary confinement, Madison showed no signs of improvement. She ate stale crackers from the cabinet, opened cans of soup and sardines and boiled plain pasta, partaking in food and beverages simply because she knew that she needed the intake in order to stay alive, although the despair she felt was so great that she questioned whether staying alive was what she wanted to do. She thought of drowning her sorrows in a bottle but realized that she didn't have one drop of liquor in her apartment and she dreaded the thought of going out.

Never before in Madison's life had she felt so lost. Even when she was drinking and partying, she always felt as though she were in control of herself. Despite what her family thought, Madison could not recall a time when she'd done one thing unwillingly. But as she sat in her darkened living room, desolate beyond comprehension, she felt as though all control had been snatched from her. After answering the phone once and speaking briefly to Liza, she ignored the ringing of both her landline and her cell phone. She informed her friend that not only did she not want to talk about what had happened, but also if she ever mentioned Steve's name again, she'd lose a friend for life.

Two days later, when Liza used her spare key to get into Madison's apartment, after banging on the door for several minutes and receiving no response, Madison rued the day that she'd ever even met her.

"Madison, your sister's been trying to reach you all day. There's something going on at home. Really, this whole thing is getting ridiculous now," Liza said, shoving Madison's feet aside and sitting down on the sofa. "And it stinks in here," she fumed.

Liza dialed Kennedy's cell phone number, ignoring Madison's pleas that she just get out of her apartment and leave her alone.

"Kennedy, I'm here in your sister's apartment and she's an absolute mess. Here she is."

"Maddie, you need to come home. It's Daddy," Kennedy said, her voice thick with trepidation.

Through the stupor she'd been in she heard the panic in her sister's voice and realized that something serious was in fact going on. With Liza's help she packed a bag, showered and booked a flight for that evening to North Carolina. Liza stayed behind cleaning Madison's apartment while she took a cab to the airport. A few hours later she landed at Douglas International Airport in Raleigh, North Carolina, and caught a taxi to Presbyterian Medical Center, where she learned that her father was in the cardiac intensive care unit. He'd suffered a massive heart attack and was listed in critical condition.

For three days, Madison, Kennedy and Elmira kept a round-the-clock vigil in the waiting room of the ICU. The three Daniels women took turns being strong and giving in to their fears. Madison could not remember ever having seen her father so weak and vulnerable. He had always been stable and dependable, a rock whose presence could be relied on every birthday, milestone, failure or success. The hospital staff allowed them to go in to see him one at a time for ten minutes every hour. It was the hardest thing Madison had ever done in her life. Sitting there watching her father fight for his life gave her a new perspective like nothing else could have. While her heart still ached terribly, she realized that she could not spend another minute mourning over what she'd lost instead of cherishing what she still had.

"Baby girl," Joseph croaked late one night while Madison sat by his side.

Madison picked up her head, her tear-streaked, exhausted face registering surprise. It was the first time her father had spoken since he'd been hospitalized.

"Daddy," Madison exclaimed, wiping the tears she'd dripped onto her father's hand, which she had been holding.

"Why are you crying all over me?" Joseph asked.

"Oh, Daddy," Madison giggled.

It was obvious that her father had managed to maintain his sense of humor through his crisis, a fact that was incredibly comforting to his youngest daughter.

"Are you all right?" Joseph asked her.

"I am now, Daddy. I am now."

After spending much of her life resisting the rigid tenets of her family, being in their midst again served to fill Madison with a renewed sense of self-pride and personal strength. She spent two weeks in North Carolina, not willing to leave until her father was out of the hospital and back home, well on the road to recovery. Drawing on her close-knit relationship with Kennedy gave Madison not only comfort, but also the resolve to view her failed relationship with Steve as a learning experience from which she benefited immensely. For a time, however brief it was, she had felt a deep, abiding love for someone and had been unselfish and giving under that love. She and Kennedy, sometimes even joined by Elmira, had long talks in which they bonded as women. Madison's icy exterior crumbled as she reached new levels of understanding about herself and the motives behind some of her past behavior. By the time she headed home, Madison was determined and rededicated to herself and to getting her priorities together.

As she moved toward truly finding her way, she knew that exorcising her heart of Stevenson Elliott wouldn't be easy, but she was determined to do so with her head held high and with no regrets.

## *Chapter 28*

The truth could be a horribly deformed and grotesquely displayed thing, especially when it sprang unexpectedly from beneath the rock under which it has been hidden for years. Steve stared at the ugly truth about the man he'd grown up admiring, respecting and revering, and the sickening sensation that invaded his stomach threatened to provoke him to heave. There was no denying the facts as they were spelled out in black and white. He slid to the floor, oblivious of the dust and grime that was settling onto the khakis he wore or the scuff marks he was making to the backs of his Italian leather shoes.

He had not intended to uncover what he'd found. In fact, after the initial search, he was not even sure of what he was looking for when he continued digging through the boxes. He'd told himself that he was still searching for insight and understanding of a father who had always seemed remote to him. He'd hoped that reading from the files he'd taken from the records room would help him, but all it ended up doing was hurting.

For a prolonged moment he wished that he could go back in time to before he pulled the red rubber band from the yellowed envelopes, because he did not know if he could ever forget the words that he'd read. Inside the envelopes, six of them in total, were letters written by his grandmother. Why they'd been stuffed in a box with company records from more than a decade before, he couldn't fathom. Each letter possessed a date that corresponded to one of the first six years after they had moved to England. They were written in April, the month he was born, and they all started in the same way—with a plea to send a birthday wish from her to him.

It was the last letter that had sucked the breath from his body as he'd read it. It was that final letter that forever shifted his recognition and understanding of his father and everything that the man stood for. In it, his grandmother expressed to her son a deep disappointment and discouragement at the man he'd grown up to be. She told him that while she understood his desire to better himself and provide for his family, she could not fathom how he could be a deceitful thief who would steal from a man who had been a brother to him for much of his life. It was that shame and disappointment that she would take to her grave.

Jonathan Morris, the man of whom she spoke, had apparently died around the time of this last letter. Jonathan had died a poor and desolate man, who in his final days had come to her and cursed her family's name. Jonathan told her that he and Gregory had had a plan for success. At a time when the industry of manufacturing bauxite was being threatened by the environmental concerns, Jonathan had discovered a way to speed up the production process at the same time decreasing the by-product discharge. He'd shared that information with Gregory, who'd advised him to keep it to himself until the time was right.

In the meantime, Gregory struck a lucrative deal using Jonathan's findings with a major mineral production company in Australia. By the time Jonathan knew what had happened, Gregory was in England. He'd taken the cash, relocated his family and was firmly planted in his position at Reynolds, making more money than Jonathan had ever seen in his lifetime. A couple of years later, Gregory had enough money to launch his own research/consultation company, Elliott Corporation, specializing in the economic and commercial aspects of the aluminum and steel industries. According to what Jonathan had told Gregory's mother, he was smart enough to cover his tracks, making it look as though the discovery was all his, thereby taking all of the credit.

Learning that his father was a liar and a cheat who had built his fortune on someone else's misfortune was a hard pill for Steve to swallow. Knowing that he'd deceived a man who had been his friend since childhood underscored the fact that no one was secure when it came to his father's lust for dominance and power. He remembered how often he'd told the story of his father's self-made success, even bragging about how industrious and diligent his father had had to be to get where he was today. He felt like a fool and there also came a profound sense of loss as he realized that everything he'd ever believed in had been shattered.

With this startling discovery came clarity as well. Now it made sense why his father never wanted to return to Jamaica and had essentially severed all ties with his homeland. He could not go back, even if he wanted to. It puzzled Steve that Jonathan Morris never came after his father. It wasn't as if he'd kept a low profile and could not have easily been found. Steve couldn't imagine what it must have been like to continue doing menial labor to feed your family while the man you'd loved and trusted like a brother wore three-piece suits to do physically undemanding work in an office.

Hours later, Steve emerged a changed man. Numbly, he returned to his flat and poured himself one glass after another of vodka, straight with no chaser. It was the strongest alcoholic beverage he had in his place and all he wanted to do was numb the gripping pain he felt in his heart. Slowly, his anger turned inward as he realized that his father was still controlling, still manipulating situations to suit his wants.

Steve cursed aloud, ramming his fist into the wall behind his front door. He'd allowed his father to ruin his future and happiness and had been pushed into turning his back on the love of his life. He'd believed that in order to be half the man his father was, he'd had no choice but to meet his demands and live under his tutelage. All the while, Gregory had spoken to him of honor and reputation, intimating that those things were of the utmost importance and suggesting that Madison was blemished in both regards. Yet it was Gregory who was the dishonorable person of questionable character. The rage that sparked and flourished inside Steve over the next few days made his thoughts blur and his ability to reason fail. A sense of panic also descended on him as he realized that he was about to compound the mistakes he'd made with another huge one.

Genevieve was everything a man could ask for in a woman. Steve thought that, in time, he could grow to love her. Yet the closer they drew to the wedding, when he should be excited by the prospect of taking a wife so beautiful and charming and the certainty that he would finally get to make love to her as her husband, he was plagued by dread.

"Steve, what do you think about these patterns?" Genevieve asked, spreading a series of colored photographs across the round oak dinette in front of Steve.

They were seated in the dining area of Steve's flat. There were six weeks remaining before the big day and Genevieve was in full throttle in the planning stages. She'd met with Janice Elliott earlier in the day and had returned home eager to share with Steve all of the progress they'd made. He tried to appear excited, working diligently to suppress the bile that rose in his throat every time someone so much as mentioned his pending nuptials. He felt as if he would burst if he didn't talk to someone, but quickly realized that there was no one he could talk to without revealing secrets that would damage, if not ruin, his father.

Three weeks before the wedding, Steve was no longer sleeping through the night. He'd go to bed exhausted and fall into a dreamless sleep. However, three or four hours later, he'd awaken, only to stare at the ceiling or pace the floor until the sun came up. He felt like he was literally going out of his mind. Sometimes he reasoned that the past months of his life had all been a cold, cruel joke and he'd waited in vain for the comedian to jump out with a resounding *gotcha.* It never happened and his despair continued. It was difficult avoiding his father. In the office he stayed behind closed doors working or pretending to. In the evenings, he spent time with Genevieve only when he could not put her off with claims of work responsibilities. Most of the time, he wandered the streets aimlessly, ignorant of the changes in weather or the people he passed on the street.

Finally, the calendar crept up on him. A few days before the wedding, he was a complete wreck. Struggling to keep his head above the quicksand in which he felt like he was sinking, he agreed to hang out with Neil. In lieu of a bachelor party, at Steve's request, Neil took him out for an evening of shooting pool and drinks.

"For a guy who is about to get married, you certainly don't look too happy. Cold feet, brother?" Neil asked.

"Not at all. I'm good." Steve smiled, taking a long swig from the ice-cold Guinness stout that Neil had just brought over from the bar.

"I hear the words, man, but I don't feel the emotion. If I were about to marry a woman as gorgeous as Genevieve, I'd be grinning and falling all over myself."

"Yeah, well, everyone's not as goofy as you are, Neil."

"Oh, okay. Take jabs at the best man if that'll make you feel better. Seriously, Steve, how long have I known you?"

"I don't know, since like the third or fourth grade. Why?"

"Well, it's like this. I've known you for two decades and you're going to stand here and tell me that you are completely okay with this wedding taking place on Saturday?"

Steve set the pint glass down on the edge of the pool table, placing both palms on the green felt and leaning over, his head hanging low. He wanted to keep up the front he'd put up. He'd been wearing a mask of happiness for so long that he'd convinced himself that he was good at it. Apparently, his mask was full of holes through which anyone who was looking could see the truth—anyone who wanted to.

"Sometimes I can't tell whether I'm coming or going these days," Steve said at long last.

"Talk to me, man," Neil said, laying his pool stick across the table.

"I've tried as hard as I know how to, pulling from deep inside to make myself believe that I was doing the right thing, but who am I kidding? I'm not doing the right thing by Genevieve or Madison."

"What about you, man? You're talking about what you're doing or not doing for everyone else but yourself."

Steve withdrew from the table, his face ashen.

"Look, Steve, I never really got in to your business when you broke up with Madison and hooked up with Genevieve. I figured you had your reasons for doing what you did. But I've got to tell you. From the moment you announced your engagement to Genevieve, I questioned your judgment. I mean, don't get me wrong, Jenny is a great girl. She's beautiful, cultured and intelligent."

"I know she's terrific," Steve agreed.

"Yeah, but I never saw you look at her or talk about her the way you did Madison. What gives?"

Steve could no longer hold it inside. All of the weeks of frustration and anger that he'd been carrying around came pouring out of him. He told Neil about his parents' ultimatum and his response. He left out any mention of his father's dirt or his mother's knowledge of it, knowing that despite how angry and disappointed he was, he could never be the catalyst for his father's ruination. He truly believed that the guilt his father possessed was eating him up, making him the hard man that he had become, and he would be worse off in the long run. Besides, he had enough regret of his own to deal with. The remorse he felt at the hurt he'd caused Madison had turned into a lump that sat in the center of his chest. He released his paralyzing fear of disobeying his parents' wishes and being forced to make his own way in life when he felt inept and unprepared to do so.

Neil listened to his friend patiently, his face an unreadable facade. When Steve had talked himself empty, he collapsed onto the hard wooden bench that lined the back wall of the pool hall. Neil joined him, silently digesting all that his buddy had shared with him.

"I bet you think I'm pretty messed-up, huh?" Steve asked, a sardonic laugh escaping his lips.

"No, no more than the rest of us. But I'll tell you this. If you don't clean this debacle up right now, you will regret it for the rest of your life."

Neil said this with a serious expression, reaching over to slap Steve on the back heartily.

"Don't you think I've thought about that? I don't know how to clean it up, man. No matter what I do, someone will be hurt. And Genevieve, she doesn't deserve this. She's been nothing but good to me. How can I walk away from her a few days before this wedding that she's spent the past two months planning?"

"True, true. That would be in extremely bad taste. On the other hand, what would it be if you marry a woman that you don't love? Look, man, I think that she can get over you if you're up front now. If you wait one, two, five years down the line, perhaps the two of you will have had children, whatever…I think it will be ten times worse. If you don't love the woman, man, then let her go. Shoot, you can hook her up with me. I'll take her mind off of you," Neil joked, giving Steve a playful shove.

Steve chewed on his friend's words all through the night and into the next day. By morning his mind was still in a fog and he moved about in a dazed stupor. He and Genevieve were scheduled to take a ten-day honeymoon to the Turks and Caicos Islands the morning following their wedding ceremony. Alone in his apartment, he began packing for this trip. He filled one suitcase with shorts and shirts, undergarments and socks. He filled a second with slacks, sweaters, suits and ties. He filled a third with shoes, sneakers and toiletries. Before he knew it, he had packed every item of clothing in his entire apartment, yet he didn't stop. He began moving quickly around from room to room. Like a man possessed, he filled cardboard boxes with books, compact discs and DVDs. He tore through his apartment like a bulldozer, and when he was finished, it appeared as though no one had ever resided there.

Steve jumped into his car, driving with the radio off and the windows rolled up tightly even though it was a warm night. It was well after dinnertime by then, and he knew that his parents would be close to retiring for the night if they hadn't done so already. That didn't matter to him because what he had to say could not wait. He arrived at the estate, barging in after using his spare key at the front

208 The Foreigner's Caress

door. He found his father in the kitchen, slicing a piece of coconut custard pie.

"Stevenson, what are you doing here at this hour? Is everything all right?"

"No, Dad, everything is not all right. Where is Mother?"

"I'm right here, dear," Janice said, appearing from the sunroom just outside the kitchen.

She held the knitting she had been doing earlier in the day as she rested on one of the chaise longues in the sun-filled room.

"What's happened?" she asked, her attention commanded by her son's obviously disturbed presence.

"I've come to tell you something, and I'd appreciate it if you would just listen to what I have to say, without commenting," Steve said.

Gregory placed the dessert slicer on the countertop beside his plate. He regarded his son with an expression that warned of intolerance. Steve ignored him, undeterred in his course of action.

"I'm not going to marry Genevieve this weekend," Steve said firmly, staring his mother directly in the eye.

"Whatever are you talking about, Stevenson? Of course you are going to marry Genevieve. Everything has been arranged. If not this weekend, then when?" Janice asked.

"No, Mother. I'm not marrying Genevieve…not this weekend and not ever," Steve responded, his tone even and deliberate.

He kept his eyes trained on his mother, unwilling to look at his father as he did not trust himself to keep a cool head.

"Stevenson, you're not making any sense. Are you feeling okay?" Janice asked worriedly.

"I've never felt better. Look, Mother, I don't love Genevieve, and I'm not going to marry her," he said, his gaze moving away from his mother's crestfallen face.

Janice's mouth dropped open and for once she was speechless.

"Son, you're not the first bridegroom to get nervous on the eve of his wedding. It's natural, but I'm sure you'll—"

"Stop talking, Dad. Just stop. All of my life I have been listening to you…hanging on your every word, trying to mirror your every action. I wanted so desperately to be like you that I never took the time out to be me or even figure out who that is. No more. Now is my time and I'm going to live my life the way I see fit."

"Stevenson, I suggest you sit down and calm yourself down. You're being emotional and irrational. Think about what you are saying, son."

"I have thought about it. I've done nothing but think about it and it doesn't matter how much time passes or how much I try to wish it away or pray it away. I love Madison Daniels, and I'm going to be with her if she'll have me. Considering how badly I've treated her, that's a long shot, but one that I'm willing to take."

"You can't do this," Janice exclaimed, having found her voice again.

"Oh, but I can and I am."

"Absolutely not! I forbid it. You are not going anywhere near that woman or—"

"Or what? Or what, Dad? Are you going to fire me? Disown me? News flash—I don't care. Madison means more to me than any job could ever. So, Dad, accept this as my formal resignation. I've packed up my entire apartment and will contact you guys when I get settled."

"Wha— Where are you going?"

"I'm going to New York to find Madison and beg her to forgive me. I'm going to figure out exactly who I am and what I'm capable of as a man."

"Dear Lord," Janice gasped as she sank down into a chair at the table.

It hurt Steve to cause his mother grief, but he knew that it was either now or later; the result would be the same.

"Mother, Dad…I thank you both for everything you've given me and every sacrifice you made for me. I know that I am alive and educated and strong because you, the two of you, made me that way. But I can't live my life for you. I have found a woman who makes me feel like I can climb mountains. Don't you see that I may never find that with anyone else? I certainly won't find it with Genevieve. I've got to go."

"You've got a hell of a lot of nerve…talking to us this way. After everything I've given you and done for you. Stevenson, if you walk out of that door, you'd better not even think about coming back," Gregory huffed.

Steve glared at his father, his rage mounting with each tick of the clock hanging on the wall behind him.

"What you've given me? What you've given? What about what you've taken?" Steve growled.

Gregory looked stunned as he stared at his son. Steve had not wanted to have this confrontation. He had hoped that he could make his announcement and be on his way, never having to acknowledge that he knew about the shameful reality of how his father had found success. Unfortunately, that wish was not to come true. Once again, the demanding person that Gregory was would not allow Steve to make a clean break without a fight.

"Jonathan Morris," Steve said.

His voice was tight when he pronounced the name. Gregory's eyes flickered only instantly, but it was enough for Steve to know that he'd struck a nerve. His father had never been a man to exhibit fear or anxiety, yet for a fleeting moment, both of those emotions registered in his eyes.

"Stevenson—" Janice began.

Steve shifted his gaze to her face. What he saw registered there was the final straw to an already cumbersome load that was weighing down on his chest and making it difficult for him to breathe. She knew.

Steve looked from his mother to his father and back to her again. Incredulity outlined his handsome face as he realized that by uttering those two words, a name that until several weeks ago had meant nothing to him, he had somehow managed to stop both of his parents in their tracks.

"How can you stand here and lecture me about all that you've given me that I should be grateful for when you stabbed your best friend in the back, took what was rightfully his and spent the last twenty years living the life he should have been living?"

His eyes were narrowed as he glared at his father. Disgusted, he turned toward his mother. "Mother, how long did you know? How could you let him do that?"

Janice didn't answer. She merely buried her face in the palms of her hands. Her sobs came in an explosion of emotion, stabbing Steve in his heart. But when he thought about what they had done twenty years ago in Jamaica, and how how they had tried to sabotage his life, he steeled himself, allowing the anger to dominate him again.

"The both of you make me sick," Steve said.

"How dare you judge us? You've lived a charmed life, thanks to me. You don't know what it's like to be poor, to have people as soon as spit on you as look at you when you pass them on the road in your tattered clothing and filth. You don't know what it's like not to eat a meal because there's only enough to feed your younger siblings. I hated that life, and I didn't give a damn what I had to do to get out of it."

Steve turned his back, not wanting to hear any explanations or give them an opportunity to finagle their way around the bomb he'd just dropped. His father's words were those of a desperate man who had been uncovered and exposed for the heartless thief that he was. Steve began walking, the sounds of his father's protests and his mother's sobs in his ears, slamming against his back as he took one step after the other. He grew more assured as he continued down the marbled corridor to the front door. He knew that he had taken the right course of action and before all was said and done, he intended to right the wrongs that had been done.

## Chapter 29

Steve left his stunned parents in the kitchen, walking out with the determination and sense of purpose that had been eluding him for months. He drove without stopping and barely seeing anything around him for the entire thirty-minute drive to where Genevieve was staying with her parents.

"Mr. Daltrey, sir, I'm sorry to disturb you at this hour," he said when the butler answered his knock and escorted him to the study where the prime minister was working.

"Nonsense. You're family now. Come in. And I told you, call me Percy. Can I get you a drink?"

Mr. Daltrey gave Steve the once-over, noticing that the young man seemed to be riled up about something. His shirt-tails hung out in the back and his eyes looked bloodshot.

"No, sir, I'm okay. Listen, I need to talk to you. I have

something to say to Genevieve, but I thought it only right if I spoke to you first."

"This sounds very serious, Stevenson."

"It is, sir. First, let me say I have the utmost respect for your daughter and for you and Mrs. Daltrey. I would never want to hurt any of you, but—"

"But what, son? What's going on?"

"Well, sir, Percy... I—I'm going to call the wedding off. I can't marry your daughter," Steve declared, his words coming out in a rush.

Steve could not measure the flood of relief that began to spread over him in increments once those words had come out of his mouth.

"Surely you're joking. The wedding is in two days. How dare you do this? Why on earth could you possibly want to do this now?" Mr. Daltrey was immediately enraged, as he calculated the embarrassment he would endure as a result of his daughter being jilted on the eve of her wedding.

"It's because he's in love with another woman, Father," Genevieve said.

She'd slipped up to the doorway of the study without either Steve or her father noticing while they were in the midst of their dialogue. She'd heard every word exchanged and now, as Steve turned to look at her, the expression on her face was unmistakably one of relief. Her bright eyes shone as she stared at Steve, her mouth a tight line. He swallowed, wishing that he could do anything to avoid hurting her but knowing that time was up.

"Genevieve, I was about to come up to see you," Steve said.

"Well, I've saved you a trip," she said evenly.

"What is this about another woman?" Percy asked testily.

"Sir, it's not even about her. I promise that I have been faithful to Genevieve the entire time I was with her," Steve said, facing the man.

He turned back toward Genevieve. "I never touched another woman from the moment you and I got together."

"I know that," she said softly.

"If this is not about another woman, then what is it about?" Daltrey said.

Percy Daltrey seemed to be having a different conversation than Steve and Genevieve. They locked eyes for a moment, neither one of them acknowledging her father's question.

"I demand to be told what the hell is going on here right now," Daltrey shouted.

"Dad, just let him go," Genevieve interjected, breaking the entanglement of their eyes.

"Genevieve, I'm sorry. I never meant to hurt you, but you deserve someone who's going to love you as much as you love him. I'm sorry I'm not that guy."

"I'm sorry, too, Steve," she said.

Genevieve's next move was one that not only shocked Steve, but made him even more certain of what a class act she was. She walked over to him and touched the side of his face lightly. Her eyes were moist yet steady as she put her arms around his body and hugged him tightly. Steve returned her embrace, whispering in her ear softly.

"Thank you," he said.

Genevieve pulled back, kissed Steve on his cheek and let him go. Her eyes were even more wet and filled with their usual brightness, but she held her head up and walked out of the room, never turning back. There was nothing left to say between them, yet it was Steve's hope that one day he'd be able to drop a line to check in on her and see how her life turned out. The question remained whether she would ever see fit to respond to him. His cowardly behavior over the past few months had caused him to hurt someone who really didn't deserve it and he had no right to expect her forgiveness. Yet he reminded himself that like Neil had said, it was better now than later.

As Steve drove away from the Daltrey estate, he realized how selfish he'd been. Being consumed by his own doubts and insecurities had led him to break two women's hearts, albeit inadvertently. He could only pray that in time, both women's hearts would heal and that one of them would allow him to love her through her pain. Once again he knew he didn't have the right to expect that, but that did not stop him from praying for it.

## Chapter 30

"All right, folks, make sure you read chapters seventeen through twenty before next class. We'll begin looking at some of the genetic factors that separate the cat family."

Madison entered the homework assignment into her Sprint PC Pal, packed her notebook, pen and handheld device into the black messenger bag propped against the side of her chair and stood. She stretched her arms above her head, her body still not quite used to sitting through two-hour lectures. She was nearing the end of her first semester at New York University and she was loving every minute of it. It still struck her as ironic that she was the same person who six years ago had dropped out of Spelman College after one year of attendance, eluding being kicked out eventually for poor academic performance. She marveled at the difference six years could make in a person's life—or even six months for that matter.

Madison pulled her red North Face jacket from the back of the chair, slipped her arms into it, and placed the strap of her bag on her right shoulder. She exited the classroom, following the stream of fellow students out of the building. The midmorning air was crisp, reminding her that winter was rapidly approaching. She was looking forward to the between semester break because she planned to spend the time in North Carolina with her parents, Kennedy and Malik. The milder temperatures were definitely something to look forward to.

Free for the day as her next class had been canceled, Madison planned to get some early Christmas shopping done before it was time for her to report to her part-time job at Parsons Veterinary Clinic. She'd only been working there for four weeks, but it was as if she'd finally landed a job that she enjoyed and learned from every single day. That night was the final night of Liza's one-woman show at Chelsea Playhouse and she'd promised to meet her friend and the play's crew at a bar near the West Twenty-second Street theater afterward for a celebratory drink. The play had done remarkably well, boasting sold-out performances for most of the sixty days it showed. It had also opened the door for Liza for even bigger and better things, including landing her a supporting actress role in an upcoming romantic comedy starring Adam Sandler, among other notable comics. Madison was so happy for her friend, whom she'd always believed to be incredibly talented.

It wasn't until Madison, who was lost in her thoughts, was about ten feet away from her car that she noticed him. Her steps slowed as she tried to comprehend the vision that was before her eyes.

"Hello, Madison," Steve said tentatively.

Although he'd rehearsed this scene a billion times in his mind, he still felt sorely unprepared for the performance of his life.

Madison sucked in a deep breath, her eyes trained on Steve's face. Outside of the goatee he was sporting, he remained unchanged. He was wearing a crisp white shirt, the collar of which could be seen beneath the navy blue pea coat he'd buttoned up to the top. Blue jeans and black Stacy Adams loafers completed his outfit. He was leaning against the driver's door of Madison's silver Ford Explorer.

"You look good," Steve said, undaunted by the lack of response he was getting from her.

Her hair had grown longer, hanging down past her ears now. The jeans she wore hugged every inch of her curvaceous bottom, and the black high-heeled boots on her slender size-six feet gave her legs an elongated look and brought her closer to his height. The cold air had colored her cheeks even though she'd only been out of doors for a few minutes. She was more beautiful than he'd remembered, even though her face had been dancing across his mind since forever.

"What are you doing here?" Madison asked finally.

"I came to see you. Your sister told me that you were taking classes over here," he said. "Please don't be angry with her. I had to beg for a full ten minutes before she conceded," he added after a shadow of disapproval passed over Madison's face.

"She shouldn't have done that."

"Please, Madison, is there somewhere we can go to talk? Just for a few minutes?" Steve asked.

Madison considered saying no, getting into her car and driving away without looking back. She thought about how many times she had dreamed that he would come to her, wanting to talk about what had happened between them and to apologize for his part in it. She'd dreamed of what she'd say and do. However, now that the moment was finally here, she could not think clearly. There were so many things that she'd wanted to say to him and so many ways in which she'd wanted to hurt him as badly as he'd hurt her. Instead, she simply led the way in silence toward the nearest coffee shop. Inside, she took a seat, refused both Steve's and the waitress' offers for a beverage and waited. Steve ordered a cup of black coffee for himself and, holding his tongue until the waitress departed, stared at Madison long and hard.

"So you're in school now?" he said.

Madison nodded her head without speaking.

"What are you studying?"

"Steve, would you please just—"

"I'm sorry. You want me to just get to the point, right? Okay, well, here's the point. Madison, I miss you."

Madison bit her bottom lip.

"You came all this way to tell me that you miss me? Hmph, I wonder what your wife thinks about that," Madison said snidely. "Did you tell her you were coming here?"

"Madison, I didn't marry Genevieve," Steve said.

Madison's eyes widened ever so slightly, but she gave no other reaction to his news.

"I couldn't go through with it," Steve continued.

When Madison still failed to speak, Steve decided to go for broke and tell her everything.

"Madison, I never loved Genevieve. She's a great person and well, I thought that if I just tried, I could somehow make a relationship work with her. It's what everyone wanted," he said.

"Not everyone," Madison responded, glaring at him.

"No, not everyone. Believe it or not, Madison, I didn't want it, either. All I ever wanted was you."

Steve reached across the table to touch Madison's hands, having wanted to touch some part of her ever since he'd first laid eyes on her that afternoon. She jerked her hand away, recoiling as if he were a poisonous snake trying to inject her with his deadly venom.

"Steve, I'm going to ask you again—why are you here?"

"I've moved here. I broke things off with Genevieve and moved here. To be with you," he said.

"Are you sure your parents will approve? I mean, they can't possibly be okay with having their little Stevenson off on his own in another country. I thought you couldn't be more than a half hour's drive out of their reach?" Madison mocked.

"I deserved that," Steve said, hanging his head.

When he looked up at her again, his eyes were bright.

"I was a coward, Madison. Nothing but a little boy playing at being a grown man. I should have stood up to my parents and made them accept you. I have no excuses for what I did, other than the fact that I was scared. My parents told me that if I continued seeing you, they would disown me. I thought that I could not make it on my own and that I needed them, when all I really needed was you. You are the one person who I can honestly say never looked at me as Gregory Elliott's son. I don't have to be anything but myself with you, and I should have trusted that, Madison. I'm so sorry that I didn't."

"Look, Steve, all of this is fine and good, and don't get me wrong, I'm happy that you're independent and doing your own thing now. However, you're not the only one who has undergone a change. I am finally happy. I'm living my life exactly the way I want to. I'm doing things for Madison, and I'm making myself happy. I'm in school, I'm working with animals and I couldn't be—"

"Yeah, I know, I know…you're happy. You couldn't be happier," Steve said. "Don't you miss me?" he asked, hitting her directly between the eyes with his pointed question.

Madison averted her eyes from Steve's, not trusting herself to look into them. "I did. For a very long time I missed you like crazy. I was sick with missing you, but, Steve, that time has passed."

Madison's jaw was firmly set, and her eyes flashed with an intensity that pierced Steve's heart. He saw that she was trying her best to be hard, and it killed him that she felt as though she had to be that way with him. "I don't believe you."

"I don't really care what you believe, Steve. I've got to go," Madison said, preparing to leave.

"Look, I've rented a studio over near Central Park South. Here are my phone numbers," he said, scratching some numbers on a napkin. "Cell and home. I know I don't have the right to ask you for anything, but if you could see it in your heart to just think about what we had…just take some time to consider if maybe we can't… Maybe there's something worth salvaging."

Madison rose slowly from the table, her heart breaking all over again as she did. It was the hardest thing she had ever done but she felt like it was the only choice she had. There was no way she could risk her heart again on Steve and come out unscathed. She ignored the napkin in his extended hand, picked up her messenger bag and walked away. The pounding of her heart in her chest was the only sound she heard as the tears streamed down her cheeks. She made a beeline back up the block toward her car.

Steve watched her retreating figure, grateful that he even had the opportunity to lay eyes on her again.

Once inside her car, Madison started the engine, her hands trembling uncontrollably. In a cruel twist of poetic justice, singer Lyfe Jennings's voice crooned through the speakers, as he sang his latest release, titled "Let's Stay Together."

With an angry snap of the wrist, she turned the power switch to the off position, unable to bear one more second of the singer's pleas to her heart.

"What are you going to do?" Kennedy asked.

"There's nothing for me to do. Steve and I are over and that's that," Madison answered.

"Right. Honey, lousy acting like that won't even get you a blue ribbon, much less an Oscar nod. Really, did you even believe yourself when you said that?"

Kennedy shifted the phone to her other shoulder, her soapy hands preventing her from holding it. When her sister called her, she had been washing the dishes left over from the masterpiece Malik had cooked the night before. He was becoming a terrific chef, but was lousy at the clean up part.

"Kennedy, how can I trust him again? I mean, what he did to me…I didn't think I was going to recover. I was so unhappy and I felt so betrayed. How can I ever trust him with my heart when I know what he's capable of doing to me? No, doing that would be stupid, and I am not a stupid woman."

"Nobody is saying that you're a stupid woman, Maddie. What you are is a human being. You have a heart and soul, you're made of skin and bones, just like everyone else. Just like Steve. He made a mistake, Madison, and I'm sure he's paid heavily for that mistake. But don't you think it's wrong to compound one mistake with another one?"

"In my mind I understand what you're saying, but in my heart…in my heart, all I can feel is the pain he caused me. I've worked so hard to push past that time and I'm doing well, Kennedy. I've finally found some balance in my life and no, I won't lie and say that I'm deliriously happy, but I'm definitely on my way there. I won't let anyone or anything undermine that."

"Not even the first man you've ever loved?"

Madison made up an excuse to end the call, unable to find the words to either contradict Kennedy's logic or express the fear she felt inside.

"Madison, have you got a couple of minutes?" Professor Logan asked. "The rest of you, have a great holiday and I look forward to seeing some of you next semester in the second section of Science Law and Policy."

The class applauded, signaling their gratitude both for Professor Logan's fine instruction and their happiness that the semester had finally drawn to a close. Madison packed her bag for the last time that semester, and hung around to see what Professor Logan wanted to speak with her about.

Professor Logan reminded Madison a lot of her father. Aside from the fact that he was a little younger than her dad, he shared some of the mannerisms she'd grown accustomed to growing up with her father. For example, he had a habit of smoothing his mustache when he was thinking, just like her father did. He also paced when he talked, slow deliberate steps that seemed to punctuate his words. Madison had liked the man right from the start and she was looking forward to taking another class with him in the coming semesters.

"Madison, I wanted to talk to you about a new program coming to the university this spring. It's an accelerated program which would allow you to get a combined degree—B.A. in natural sciences and master's in a specialized discipline. You'll be able to do this in four academic years as opposed to six. I think you would be an excellent candidate for it. You're tenacious and inquisitive. I think you will make a fantastic veterinarian and the sooner we get you trained, the better."

"Wow, Professor Logan, I don't know what to say. I have to be honest with you though…I really don't know if I'm up to the challenge. It's taken me a long time to even decide to come back to school at all. This has been a year of adjustments for me," Madison confessed.

"Why don't you just take some time to think about it? You wouldn't need to apply until the beginning of next semester. Go home and discuss it with your family and let me know what you decide. Remember, it's a great opportunity, but it will require a major time commitment and a tremendous amount of work."

"I understand, Professor Logan, and thank you very much for thinking of me," Madison said, shaking the professor's hand.

Madison floated out of the classroom, elated by the professor's faith in her. No one had ever expressed that amount of confidence in her academic abilities. Perhaps it was because she'd never shown much interest or diligence before now. Whatever the reason, it made her feel good to know that she was so supported. However, she wasn't sure that she was up to the challenge of continuing on for three years of medical school after completing her bachelor's degree.

She headed home, planning to get her laundry done and pack for her trip home. She intended to get on the road by dawn the following morning and had a lot to do between now and then. She refused to acknowledge this, but the fact was that one of the reasons she was so eager to head down to North Carolina was that being in the same city for the past month with Steve was emotionally exhausting. It wasn't just his weekly extravagant flower deliveries or the daily voice mail messages he left for her. It wasn't even the fact that she'd spotted him sitting in a parked car outside her apartment on more than one occasion or that he'd called both Kennedy and Elmira several times to apologize, asking them to talk to Madison on his behalf. What caused her the most angst was having him physically so near, but feeling like there were oceans between them. She was sure that her boat had too many holes in it to carry her safely to him.

"Excuse me, Miss Daniels?" a voice called from behind.

Madison turned to find a man dressed up like a big orange sun, skinny white legs sticking out from beneath the costume, standing on the curb.

"Yes?" she asked, her eyebrows knotted in confusion.

"I have a singing telegram for Miss Madison Daniels,"

"What? Oh no, really that's quite all right…. No,

stop…please," Madison shouted, bursting out in laughter in spite of herself as he continued to sing. "Here, I'll pay you to stop," she said.

She reached into her purse and pulled out a twenty-dollar bill, which she thrust into the off-key heat source's hands.

"All right, suit yourself. Here, I was also supposed to give you this," he said, reaching into an opening on the side of his costume and handing Madison a small box.

The ringing telephone greeted Madison as she fumbled with the package, her bag and her keys at her front door. She stumbled into the apartment and snatched up the telephone. There was nothing that could have prepared her for the voice on the other end of the line.

"Hello?"

"Good day. Is this Madison Daniels?"

"Yes. Who's calling?"

"Hello, dear. This is Janice Elliott. Did I catch you at a bad time?"

Madison's jaw dropped, the phone trembling in her hand. She released everything she was carrying onto the sofa.

"Hello? Madison, are you still there?" Janice asked.

"Yes…uh, yes, I'm here."

"Good, good. Do you have a minute? I'd really like to talk to you about something."

"Uh, well, I'm actually a little busy and uh, I just walked in—"

"Please, Madison. It will only take a minute," Janice persisted in what was her best attempt at humility.

Madison slid down onto the sofa next to her belongings, curiosity over what Janice Elliott could possibly have to say to her outweighing her disdain for the woman.

"Fine. What can I do for you?" she asked.

"No, dear, it's more a question of what I can do for you," Janice said, her characteristic haughtiness resurfacing.

"With all due respect, Mrs. Elliott, there is nothing on this earth that you can do for me," Madison snapped.

"Just hear me out, please. I'm calling to say something to you that I should have said a long time ago—I was wrong."

Madison froze, words once again eluding her. She looked around her apartment, waiting for the guy with the camera to jump out and tell her that she'd just been cranked. Surely this had to be some kind of joke.

"I know that you're probably thinking that this is some sort of hoax, but I assure you, I am sincere," Janice said as if reading her mind. "I have had a lot of time to think about this whole affair, especially since Stevenson left home, and I know now that I was wrong to have interfered in his life. He is a grown man, and he should have been able to choose the person he wanted to spend his life with without my or his father's meddling. It wasn't fair to him or to you."

"Wow, Mrs. Elliott, I really don't know what to say. I know how difficult making this call must have been for you and I do appreciate it."

"No, it wasn't difficult at all because it is the right thing to do. You have to understand that all I've ever wanted was the best for my son. He's my only child and it is my job to make sure that he has nothing but good in his life. However, I also know that I've raised a wonderful, intelligent young man. I should have trusted him when he told us that you were a good woman."

Madison touched her face to find it wet with tears that

she had not known she was shedding. She wiped her face, overcome by the sincerity of Janice's words.

"I really do appreciate your calling, Mrs. Elliott. I wish that things had gone differently. Maybe I could have handled the situation better, too."

"You sound like you've given up hope, dear."

"Mrs. Elliott, it's over between your son and me. Steve made a choice and now we've all got to live with it, like it or not."

"Sweetheart, let me tell you something. I've made a lot of choices in my life, good and bad. I've learned that it's never too late if you are serious about wanting to change. My son loves you, Madison. He's a good man and he has decided for himself that without you in his life, nothing else matters. He has walked away from a future that was essentially paved in gold, willing to risk it all in order to win you back. Right now things are still very strained between Mr. Elliott, Stevenson and me, and I don't know if we will ever repair the damage that we've done to our relationship. I do know this—it is not too late for you and my son to heal each other. Don't let a sense of false pride get in your way, dear."

Madison said goodbye to Mrs. Elliott, thanking her again for her call but making no promises. She sat silently contemplating all of the unexpected events of the day, her mind reeling from all that had occurred. When she finally remembered the package the sun guy had given her, she tore it open in quiet anticipation. Inside she found Steve's grandfather's medallion. The note he'd written and tucked inside the velvet box was simple.

Hold on to this for me. I'm going home to find the rest of me. Yours forever, Steve.

Steve answered the telephone on the first ring. At the sound of Madison's voice, his senses came alive again, as if awakening from a deep sleep. He fell to his knees, believing that he had nothing but divine intervention to thank for bringing Madison back to him.

# Chapter 31

The three days Steve and Madison spent in North Carolina was a healing time for their relationship as well as an opportunity for them to do some of the talking that should have been done a long time before. While Joseph and Elmira Daniels opened their arms and their hearts to Steve, they were still not quite ready to forgive his parents for their treatment of Madison. However, at Madison's insistence they held their tongues about it. If they'd learned nothing else over the years, it was that meddling in their daughters' affairs would guarantee them a one-way ticket out of their lives.

"Steve, I can respect what you've given up in order to be with my daughter. However, I do question whether you will one day blame her for that very thing," Joseph said.

He and Steve were out on the tennis court behind the main house. It was the afternoon of Christmas Eve and it was a warm sixty degrees. They had just finished a game in which the elder man had put on a great display, hardly showing any evidence that just a short time ago he'd suffered a heart attack. Joseph participated in some sort of physical activity at least four days out of seven each week, determined to keep himself in the best shape possible.

"I understand what you're saying, sir, and it's a fair statement for you to make. But Madison never asked me to give up anything. I did it for me as much as I did it for her. I'm just grateful that she was able to forgive me for not doing it sooner," Steve replied.

"That's good enough for me, young man. So, now that you are unemployed, what are your plans?"

"I'm still trying to figure that part out. I have an MBA and a very good head for corporate operations, but all I've ever done is work at the Elliott Corporation—very limited experience, I know. I think I'd like to shift gears, you know? Perhaps do something that will have some sort of an impact on someone else's life. I mean, like in your practice, you touch real people and effect change in people's everyday lives. That's got to be an awesome experience."

"Well, I say trust your instincts. You're young…don't let anyone tell you that there isn't still time for you to do what you want to do with your life. Believe me, when I was laid up in that hospital, I thought surely that my number was up. But the good Lord saw fit to give me another chance and I promised myself that I was going to make the most of it. Travel a little bit more, spend more time with the family…I was even thinking about spending some time teaching at that youth center Malik's got going in D.C. Bottom line is, life's too short not to make the most of it."

Just then Madison appeared on the back porch, carrying a tray of tall glasses of lemonade.

"I can't argue there," Steve said as he stared at her, still overwhelmed by the knowledge that it could have been Genevieve standing there beckoning to him, instead of the woman he loved.

Later that evening as Steve and Madison packed their belongings in preparation for a quick return to New York and then a flight in two days to Jamaica, Madison gave him some information that both surprised and warmed him.

"I didn't tell you this before, because I wasn't sure how you'd react."

"What's up? You can tell me anything," Steve said.

"Your mother called me...the day you sent the singing telegram."

Steve bristled at the mention of his parents. He had told Madison everything he'd learned about them and had gone in to detail about the fight he'd had with them. He'd spoken to his mother only twice since he'd been in New York; not at all to his father. He was still having a hard time resolving his feelings about them and even though he hated being estranged, he needed more time to sort through things. He was hoping that his trip to Jamaica helped him heal in a way that would allow him to forgive and forget.

"What did she say to you?" he asked.

"Basically, she apologized for her part in our breakup. She gave us her blessing," Madison said.

Steve thought for certain she was joking, but her serious countenance told him otherwise. Just when he thought he could not be caught off guard by anything else, his mother had fooled him again.

"I know you're angry with them, Steve, but you know, life is too short to hold on to grudges. You never know what's going to happen. Maybe you should call them…try to talk things out with them," she said.

"You're the second person today to say something to that effect to me," Steve said, pulling her into his arms.

"Well, great minds think alike," she said, kissing him sweetly on his lips.

He'd wanted to make love to her from the moment they'd reunited. However, he also wanted to wait until the time was right. They'd rushed in to a relationship before, hardly taking the time to consider what they were doing and the bumps that lay ahead of them. Not this time. This time, he was going to make sure there would be no obstacles or stumbling blocks that would derail their train. For starters, he needed to settle the turmoil of his conscience and find a way to make peace about his grandmother and the rest of his family. He knew that that included his parents, too, but his forgiveness would come in due time. Right now, he felt fueled by Madison's commitment to establishing her own self-truths. He was determined to pursue his long-felt desire to reconnect with the extended family his parents had isolated him from. He was prepared to go home to put his demons to rest so that he could move forward with his life.

Steve and Madison rode through the bumpy hills of St. Elizabeth in silence. They held hands as they stared out of the SUV at the magnificent countryside. Steve's stomach was a tangled mass of nerves, but he also felt deep within his marrow that he was doing the right thing, no matter what the outcome. He had inquired about the Elliotts of St. Elizabeth, only to be informed that many of them had moved into the bigger parishes of Montego Bay and Negril, but that a few of them remained out in the country. Steve searched the countryside as they rode, trying to grasp at the memories of his childhood that had for a long time been part of his every waking moment, but had somehow over the years grown fuzzier and less focused until they disappeared. The country held a vague familiarity for him, but there was nothing he could point to distinctly and recall having seen before.

The driver turned onto a small graveled road, driving slowly past a white gate that was in need of repair. He pulled the car to a stop in front of a modest ranch-styled home that was brightly painted.

"Dis 'ere is Burton Elliott's house. Him de oldest of the Elliotts in dis area that me know 'bout."

Steve thanked the driver and got out. He'd paid the man to remain with them at least for the day, as they were uncertain where they'd end up. Steve walked up to the front door as Madison climbed out of the vehicle.

"Eh, mon…lost ya way?"

The man who'd opened the door was about sixty. He was thin, but stood very erect in his brown slacks and light blue short-sleeved cotton shirt.

"Good morning, sir. I was looking for the relatives of Elvin and Mirna Elliott," Steve said.

"And you ah who?"

"I'm Stevenson Elliott. I'm their grandson. I've just arrived here from England, and uh, well, I haven't been back home to Jamaica in a number of years…twenty-three to be exact. I'm not sure where anyone is," Steve said, feeling like a little boy being interrogated by one of the stern schoolmasters of his youth.

"Stevie? Stevie, is you dat? Oh, Lord, me long fe see you Stevie…Julie, Julie, woman, come see," the man began yelling.

In a sudden moment of clarity Steve recognized the man and his heavy patois accent.

"Uncle Nevel?" he asked in amazement.

"Yes, child, ah me mon! Ah me."

Uncle Nevel stepped farther outdoors, grabbing Steve by his shoulders and giving them a firm shake as if to make sure that he wasn't imagining the whole thing. At that moment, a woman came out onto the porch.

"Lord have mercy, praise God. Lickle Stevie gone big now," she said.

"Stevie, you remember Julie? Julie was my steady girlfriend back when you was a lickle bwoy. Me used to take you down de road when me ah visit with her sometime. She always spoiled you and give you too much sweetie candy and ting. Make you bounce around like a pot of jumping beans."

"Hello, Miss Julie. It's nice to see you again," Steve said politely, racking his brain to draw up a memory of her.

"Who dis lovely young lady?" Nevel said, turning toward Madison, who was leaning against the back of the vehicle.

Madison wiped at the tears that had formed in her eyes as she watched Steve reconnect with his family.

"This is my fiancée, Madison Daniels."

"Come 'ere, child," Julie said.

Taking Madison by the hand she said, "Ooh, Stevie. She's a pretty ting, eh, Nevel?"

"Yah man, Stevie found himself a nice lickle jubie."

"Come in, come in. Get out of all the sun," Julie said.

"True ting, come in."

Steve and Madison followed the couple into the house. Nevel ushered them into the parlor.

"Rest pon the setting dere." Nevel smiled, motioning to the floral-print sofa.

"Me ah go mek someting good," Julie said, rushing off to the kitchen.

"Uncle Nevel, I can't believe I found you so fast. I asked about you in Black River parish and no one was too sure. They said you'd moved away from here a long time ago."

"Me did, me did so. Me got work for a producer over in Kingston. Did some engineering work and ting for a number of years. Julie and me come back dis way a few months ago to look in 'pon Burton. You remember Burton? Him ah me and your father uncle."

"No, I don't remember him," Steve said, shaking his head slowly.

"No, you might not. 'Em was away when you were a baby…'em was in de States back den, but 'em did get inna lickle trouble and come back home. Yeah, you were gone a England by the time 'em come back. Anyway, 'em suffering so now…throat cancer eating at 'em."

"Oh, I'm sorry to hear that."

"Yeah, well, we all have to meet our maker someday. All you can do is hope that you've done the right tings in your life so that when you meet 'em, 'em ah go feel merciful, know wha me a say?"

"Yes, Uncle Nevel, I do. I guess that's part of the reason why I'm here," Steve said.

Uncle and nephew exchanged looks that said that it was time for them to talk real talk.

"Excuse me, gentlemen, but I'm going to go and see if I can help Miss Julie in the kitchen. Uncle Nevel, can you direct me?" Madison said.

She squeezed Steve's shoulder as she moved past him.

"Sure, darling. Just go straight down de hallway until you nah go anymore. It's 'pon de righthand side."

Steve looked around the cozy room, modestly furnished with a pine wood coffee table in front of the couch and matching end tables on either side. Uncle Nevel sat in an over-stuffed arm chair studying Steve as he surveyed the room.

"What's on your mind, son?" Uncle Nevel said at last.

Steve let out a breath, his gaze resting on his uncle's face. It was hard for him to believe that more than two decades had passed since he'd last seen his uncle. He almost didn't recognize him. In fact, he hadn't. Uncle Nevel had been his favorite of all the uncles. No matter how hard he'd worked in the fields, he'd never been too busy to hoist him up on his shoulders for a ride or to teach him how to pitch rocks in the pond or to climb a coconut tree and pick the ripest fruit from it.

"I feel like there's a part of me that I just don't know and never will. It's like when we moved to England, my parents and I... For them, life started right there, but for me, there was always something missing. I don't under-stand my father and his views, Uncle Nevel, and maybe I never will, but unlike him, I just couldn't stay away. There are things that I need to know about my family, our history, in order for me to find my way. Does that make any sense at all?" Steve said.

"Son, your 'istory is who you are. Without a clear understanding of dat, you cannot possibly understand where you're going in de future. You're not wrong to want to know dat part of your family tree dat you were kept away from. But son, what me want fe know is what has your father told you about his family?"

"I'm ashamed to admit that he hasn't told me much. He was very angry when I confronted him…before I left England. He feels like I should just let the past stay in the past," Steve said.

"And you? What do you feel?"

Uncle Nevel leaned forward expectantly, as if he had been waiting for this moment, this very conversation for a very long time and now that it was here, he did not want to miss one word of it. Steve studied the creases in his uncle's brown, round face, the yellowing of his deep-set eyes that made him look like a fat owl. The hands of time had caressed this man, gently pushing him toward the twilight of his life. A deep pang of guilt and a sense of loss hit Steve in the center of his heart as he was reminded of the number of years that had been lost between him and this part of his family. He was determined not to let his parents' decisions continue to cheat him of the richness of and connection to his history.

"I feel that I have a right to know where I come from and who I come from. Whether or not my parents support my decision, I'm here and I want to know you guys," Steve said.

Uncle Nevel watched Steve as he spoke, listening to his words but also reading the language of his body and the sincerity in his eyes.

"Come wid me," Uncle Nevel said.

He rose slowly from the sofa, taking a moment to press the palm of his hand against his back before straightening fully to a standing position. He led Steve down the hallway, past the kitchen, the bathroom and a bedroom, before opening the door to a bedroom at the far end of the hall. He turned on a floor lamp, moved into the room and opened a closet door. Steve watched with growing curiosity as he wandered what his uncle could possible have that would be of value or want for him.

"Sid down," Nevel called from inside of the closet.

Steve took a seat on the day bed that was covered with a green floral comforter. The room smelled like an old person's and once again Steve was reminded that almost a quarter of a century had passed since he'd departed Jamaica and left behind the people who'd once seemed invincible to him. Uncle Nevel grunted as he struggled to remove something from the closet. Steve was about to ask the man if he needed his help when Nevel suddenly emerged from the closet, carrying a small personal safe in his wrinkled hands. He placed the safe on the bed beside Steve and sat down to begin working at its combination lock.

"Now, let's see…the number is four, twenty-two, seventy-seven," Uncle Nevel said, his arthritic fingers slowly turning the dial.

"That's my birth date," Steve remarked.

"So it is," Nevel said, looking up briefly with a twinkle in his eye.

The lock turned, clicking each time Nevel landed on the correct number. After the last turn of the dial, the door sprang open.

"Your grandmother kept some tings in here. Me tink it's time these tings dem went to the rightful owner."

Nevel reached into the safe and pulled out a couple of yellowed photographs, which he handed over to Steve. The first one was of Steve and his grandmother. He was about three years old and she was holding him on her hip while she stood over a washbasin as she prepared to give him his evening bath. Steve smiled as he laid eyes on his grandmother for the first time in over twenty years. He ran his finger over the picture, wanting to feel her touch once again. Disappointed, he placed the photograph on the bed beside him and studied the second picture. This one was of him and another boy. He was about four years old and the boy standing by his side with his arm draped around Steve's shoulder was a few years older, appearing to be eight or nine.

"I don't remember this. Is this a cousin or something?" he asked.

Nevel didn't say anything. He merely pulled a folded piece of paper from the safe and handed it to Steve.

Steve opened the worn ivory writing paper and immediately recognized the writing as his grandmother's. It matched the writing of the letters he'd found back at his parents' place a few months before. Once again, his grandmother was reaching out from the beyond and he braced himself for what startling news she would deliver this time. He read the letter once, then again, unable to absorb what was being disclosed. He looked up at his uncle, whose face confirmed what the words he'd read said. He picked up the photograph of himself and the other boy whom he'd believed to be a cousin.

"My brother?" he asked, his voice shaky.

"Yeah, mon, 'em ah ya broda. His name is Alexander and 'em was born five years before you. His mother was a woman named Patricia Morris. She was married to Jonathan Morris."

"Jonathan Morris?" Steve said, stunned.

"Yes. 'Em was a good friend of your father's."

"I know…I know who he was. What…I—I don't understand this. How could he be my brother?"

"Well, me nuh know all of the particulars, but after Mama died, me go tru all of she belongings dem and the safe and me found the letter. It seems Patricia came to she a few years after you guys ah go to foreign. Jonathan was in a really bad way…'em got caught up in a lot of stuff like drugs, petty crime and tings. Anyway, Patricia was sick. She had cancer and she nah tink she had long to live. She came to Mama and told her that Alexander was really Gregory's child and that no one knew it. It seems she had been hiding de truth that she and Gregory had carried on behind Jonathan's back for all those years. Long story short, Mama agreed to keep Alexander, who by then was almost a teenager. She promised she would raise him up to be a man, but that she would never tell anyone de truth, if that is what Patricia wanted."

"I can't believe this."

Tears welled up in Steve's eyes. What had started out as a pilgrimage home to find some peace of mind had led to a punch in the gut from which he was unsure whether or not he would recover.

"Me know it is a lot to take in at one time, but it's long past time that you knew."

"Did my parents know…I mean, did my father know?"

"Me don't tink so. Me tink that was the way Patricia

wanted it. When Alexander came to live with Mama, 'em never knew that she was really his grandmother, but she loved that bwoy and raised him up, just like she promised. When she died, Alexander went to Canada to attend school. 'Em ended up staying there and worked on films and such there for a number of years. Now 'em have a house on the other side of the island in Montego Bay and 'em divide his time between Canada and Jamaica."

"And he still doesn't know?"

"Not as far as me know. Me talk to 'em from time to time and 'em doing well. 'Em happy…have a wife now and a lickle bwoy, too. Me 'ave his number around 'ere if you'd like it."

Steve wiped at the tears that had begun falling onto his cheeks. He nodded his head slowly.

"Yes, I would," he said.

A short while later they rejoined Madison and Julie in the living room. They stayed for refreshments and talked well into the evening. On the ride back to their hotel, Steve showed Madison the photograph and the letter. As he had already filled her in on the discoveries he had made about his father, she continued to encourage him to find a way to reconcile himself with what he'd discovered now with this new information. With his having spent all of his life feeling lonely and alone as an only child, learning that he had a brother immediately filled him with a sense of companionship. He couldn't wait to call him and introduce himself. He would wait to talk to his parents until after he'd had an opportunity to speak with Alexander. It was safe to say that this would be a shock for everyone involved.

Back in their hotel room, Steve contemplated making

the phone call to his brother right then and there, but there was another, equally pressing issue that had been bombarding him all day along. He didn't think he could spend one more minute around Madison without tearing all of her clothing off her and making passionate love to her. She went into the bathroom to take a shower and he paced in front of the closed door like a caged lion before deciding that he had to have her. He removed all of his clothing and moved into the room, shutting the door to the steamy tropical paradise with its potted palm trees and colorful island décor. Madison heard him enter and merely stepped aside to make room for him in the shower stall. She had been willing him to her and, therefore, was not caught off guard by his sudden appearance.

She dropped her head down toward her chest as the warm water ran down her neck and back. From behind her, Steve filled the sponge again with warm water by holding it beneath the forceful water spewing from the shower head, squeezed it out over the back of her body and watched it run down her back, over the plump hills of her luscious behind. He bent his head, allowing his lips to press against the smooth flesh of her shoulder blades. Her skin felt hot to his touch, the heat within her radiating outward. He reached around her body and placed his hands on her breasts, while his mouth continued to taste her back and the nape of her neck beneath her now wet locks of hair. He moved closer to her, so that now the water was glancing off the side of his body. Madison placed both hands against the cool tiles of the shower stall and leaned forward so that the lower half of her body was pressed against his. Steve shuddered and groaned when his stiff member made contact with her curvy rear. It had been so long since he'd felt the grace and beauty of her body against his. He could not count how many times he'd dreamed of having her again, but he recalled vividly how tortured those months had been and how he'd physically ached for her.

In a sudden and forceful movement, he spun Madison around and moved in closely, until her back was against the wall and he was inches from her. His breath filled her nostrils as he breathed heavily in her face. He lowered one hand to her left outer thigh, kneading the flesh as if it were freshly floured dough waiting to be softened for baking. Her wet skin was slick against his palm as she raised her leg, sliding the inner part of her thigh up against the outside of his. Madison raised her arms above her head in surrender and when Steve grasped both of her wrists in one of his hands, holding her captive, she realized that she was in for the sweetest torture imaginable. She braced herself, her excitement threatening to weaken her knees and drop her to the bottom of the shower stall.

"I thought I'd never get to touch you like this again. It was almost too much to bear," Steve said.

"I'm here, baby, and I'm not going anywhere," Madison replied breathlessly.

She covered his mouth with hers, wanting to crawl inside his body, to get so deep that there would be one where there used to be two. Steve's mind raced with thoughts of all of the things he wanted to do to her and with her. The ways in which he planned to enjoy her were endless, filling him with wild and impatient desire. His rod was as hard as a diamond, jutting against her belly as he kissed her. She placed one foot on the soap rest, her legs opening wide to give him access to her waiting nest. But he made her wait. He wanted to extend their time together for as long as possible. His tongue circled her collarbone as he sucked and lapped at every part of her within reach. She leaned forward, pressing her center against him in demand. He didn't want her to do that, knowing that he could not resist her sexy moves.

"Stop teasing me," she whispered.

Her command was much too powerful for him to resist any longer. Like an obedient soldier, he bowed to her desire with an overwhelming fervor to please. He penetrated her swiftly, too eager to take his time. The warmth of her vault welcomed him like an old friend, closing its door tightly around him as if she never intended to let him leave.

Their gasps and moans were replaced by screams of sheer delight. Steve released Madison's arms in order to lift her into the air and drive his wand home more deeply. She encircled his neck, gripping him to her as she rode wave after wave of pleasure. There was no end in sight to their reunion, as neither one of them could fathom growing tired of renewing their carnal knowledge of one another. They moved from the shower to the marble countertop to the floor. Their lovemaking was raw and demanding, and they each strove to answer the other's commands.

"Steve, St-e-e-eve," she sang in a harmony so melodious to his ears that he wished he could record it to play it back over and over again.

"I love you," he grunted in her ear, his tongue toying with her earlobes and tracing a trail down the side of her face.

He thrust inside her, withdrew the length of himself until only the tip remained in her treasure and then thrust himself fully into her again. The ripples of pleasure that stole through her body were immense.

"I never stopped loving you," she responded, giving back as good as she got.

"Tell me again. Tell me you love me, Madison. Tell me you're never going to leave me," Steve said.

"I love you so much, baby. I…I…oh, Steve, I love you," she whined.

She dug her nails into his back, causing a shot of painful pleasure to pierce his body. Madison's toes flexed and her shapely legs shook as she reached a climax that was riveting and unparalleled to any she'd ever felt before. Steve joined her, exploding in a burst of color and brilliance, their voices joined together in a symphony of bliss. Madison knew then, as if she had never been confused about it, that lovemaking with the one you loved more than life itself was the most gratifying experience one could ever obtain. She held on to her man, her love, her life while their bodies convulsed and, eventually, quieted.

It was uplifting to know that the trials and tribulations they'd endured were merely preparation for a lifetime of loving toward which they headed eagerly. The growth that they'd each achieved since the time they'd met had been phenomenal, but what struck her more was the fact that she was willing to continue to grow and move forward by his side. Gone was the spoiled, impulsive girl of a few years prior. In her place was a woman who finally knew her value and her identity. She also knew what she wanted out of life and how hard she was willing to work to get it.

Madison, whose eyes had been closed, opened them to find a smiling Steve studying her.

"You were a million miles away just now," he observed.

"No, baby, I was right here. I was just thinking that there is no other place that I'd rather be than here, with you. I'm going to stay here for as long as you want me…even longer. We'll spend our days building a home and our nights making love. We'll get to know your brother and his family and we'll rediscover your home together."

"And in between, we'll make babies…lots of babies who will all look just like you. And they'll know that they're loved, no matter what they do," Steve said.

"Is this all really happening, Steve? It's so hard for me to believe that we're really here, together. I had given up hope," Madison said.

"Shh, don't say that. Don't ever say that. This is very real…we are real and our future together is real. I'm home, Madison, and with you by my side I know that I can do anything I set my mind to do. With you, I'll always be home. I want you to be my wife, Madison, and I want you to have my children. I want you to grow old with me, fight with me and make up with me."

Madison studied the earnestness in his face and knew that despite all that had happened between them, they were exactly where they were meant to be at the time they were supposed to be there.

"I do," she said before pulling Steve's face to hers.

She kissed his mouth gently, his face between the palms of her hands. What had begun as a foreign affair had evolved into a bond that spoke the universal language of love. The sweet smell of mangos wafted in through the window of their suite, paling in comparison to the delectable fragrance of their union.

# *Epilogue*

"Dr. Elliott, Mrs. Reese is on the line. She wants to know if she can bring Boscoe over right now. She said that he can't keep anything down. I told her you were preparing to leave for the day, but she sounds frantic," the office assistant said.

"Thanks, Nancy. Tell her to bring him right in," Madison replied.

She retrieved the lab coat she'd just hung on the back of her office door and slipped her arms back into the garment. She picked up her cell phone from the desk and hit the number one on the speed dial. Steve picked up on the first ring.

"Hey, baby. Are you on your way home?" he asked.

"Not exactly. I've got a sick puppy coming in on an emergency visit, so I'm going to be here a little while longer," she answered.

"You and your sick puppies," Steve scolded.

"I know, but Boscoe's so cute and fluffy...how can I resist him?"

"I'm cute and fluffy, too, and so is this little guy right here," Steve said, hoisting their six-month-old son, Stevie, from his playpen. "Say 'hi, Mommy'," he cooed.

"Oh, sweetie, Mommy's coming home very soon," Madison said at the sound of her son's gurgling into the telephone. "Babe, should I pick up something for dinner?"

"Nope, I've got it covered. I made your favorite," Steve replied.

"Man, what am I going to do when you go back to teaching at the school? No more home-cooked meals and bubble baths when I get home," Madison lamented.

"Not to worry. I'll always take care of you," Steve promised.

"I know," Madison said, hanging up with the assuredness that comes with a love built as solidly as they come.

It was still hard for her to believe how time had flown since she'd first met Steve. The love they felt for each other was made stronger every day by their open communication and vow to put each other first above all else. Their wedding had been a lavish affair in the backyard of a beautiful church in Jamaica. It had been attended by much of her family and most of his, with the exception of his father. While Steve and Gregory had since built a fragile bridge, they still had miles to walk before they got to a place with each other that was unguarded.

Steve's profession was as a business and economics teacher at an all boys' charter school in Manhattan and he loved every minute of it. He had taken a six-month sabbatical to stay at home with their son after Madison returned to her veterinary practice. Working with her animal friends gave Madison the sense of fulfillment she'd been longing for and her pride in her accomplishment was greater than she'd imagined it could be. She had celebrated her thirtieth birthday on the same day that their son, her greatest success, was born. The headstrong, wild child she had once been had morphed into a woman who people still loved to talk about—only now they did so with admiration.

# Two GROOMS and a Wedding

### Award-winning author
## Adrianne Byrd

For one forbidden night, ambitious attorney
Isabella Kane indulged her deepest passions.
Now she can't get Derrick Knight out of her mind...
and Derrick is equally obsessed. The problem is,
Isabella's engaged to his old college rival.
But Derrick's determined to make Isabella his.

"A humorous, passionate love story."
—*Romantic Times BOOKreviews*
on *Comfort of a Man* (4 stars)

*Coming the first week of March, wherever books are sold.*

**KIMANI**
ROMANCE

"Ms. Craft is a master at storytelling…"
—*Romantic Times BOOKreviews* on *Star Crossed*

Author favorite

# Francine Craft

# Designed
for
# PASSION

*Second chances never looked so good…*

When Melodye Carter's husband's mysterious death is linked to another shooting, Detective Jim Ryman must protect Melodye and her twin boys. Jim shut down his heart after losing his wife, but proud, vulnerable Melodye makes him remember what it means to be a man in love.

*Coming the first week of March, wherever books are sold.*

KIMANI™
ROMANCE

**www.kimanipress.com**    KPFC0570308

# A
# RISKY
# AFFAIR

Award-winning author

## Maureen Smith

Private investigator Dane Roarke leaves Solange Washington
breathless with desire. Hired to do a routine background
check on her, Dane unearths secrets regarding her parentage
that force him to walk a thin line between his growing
suspicions and his consuming hunger for this vibrant woman.

"*With Every Breath* [by Maureen Smith] is engaging reading
that is sure to provide hours of pleasure."
—*Romantic Times BOOKreviews*

*Coming the first week of March, wherever books are sold.*

KIMANI
ROMANCE™

**www.kimanipress.com**          KPMS0590308

# WHEN LOVE Calls

### National bestselling author

# CELESTE O. NORFLEET

Washington lobbyist Alyssa Wingate is tired of all the double-talk surrounding the plight of the elderly, and is determined to do something about it. So she sets her sights on obtaining the help of Senator Randolph Kingsley, a man of enormous popularity and power. But will their mutual attraction get in the way of advancing her cause... and his career?

"Norfleet's latest is sinfully sexy reading with a hint of mystery and a dash of humor."
—*Romantic Times BOOKreviews* on *Only You*

**Coming the first week of March,
wherever books are sold.**

### ARABESQUE®

**www.kimanipress.com**

KPCON110308

These women are about to discover that every passion
has a price...and some secrets are impossible to keep.

# NATIONAL BESTSELLING AUTHOR
# ROCHELLE ALERS

## *After Hours*

A deliciously scandalous novel that brings together
three very different women, united by the secret lives
they lead. Adina, Sybil and Karla all lead seemingly
charmed, luxurious lives, yet each also harbors a
surprising secret that is about to spin out of control.

"Alers paints such vivid descriptions that when Jolene
becomes the target of a murderer, you almost feel
as though someone you know is in great danger."
—*Library Journal* on *No Compromise*

**Coming the first week of March
wherever books are sold.**

*sepia*™

**www.kimanipress.com**          KPRA1220308